MW01196545

Advance praise for

The Payback

"Cauley burnishes her page-turner with shrewd commentary on the debt burden placed on first-generation college students. It's a knockout."

—*Publishers Weekly*

"Could this novel be any more timely or more delightful? Delicious, fabulist, and cuttingly insightful about the current moment, *The Payback* is *Moonstruck* meets heist movie, true fun with real teeth. We will all be reading Cauley for many years to come."

—Rufi Thrope, author of *Margo's Got Money Troubles*

"*The Payback* is as shady, cunning, and wickedly fun as its gimlet-eyed narrator. It describes—like nothing else—an America drowning in cheap merch and dipping FICA scores, the endless want of living here. Luigi, save us. We know not what we've done."

—Danzy Senna, author of *Colored Television*

"A bold, fast-paced novel that blends the thrills of a heist with an incisive critique of the modern politics of debt. With razor-sharp wit and unforgettable heroes, this subversive tale of rebellion and reinvention cements Cauley's place as a masterful voice in modern fiction."

—Lauren Wilkinson, author of *American Spy*

"A novel of great fun and unforgettable fury, *The Payback* sharply questions the punitive systems we live within, the contradiction between social well-being and individual wellness, and what it means to work toward a decent life."

—Megha Majumdar, bestselling author of *A Burning*

"An exciting and hilarious heist novel that centers down-on-their-luck older millennials who are riddled with debt and decide to take matters into their own hands to dismantle the system. Timely and witty, Cauley's plotting, prose, and character development will keep you hooked from start to finish."

—Morgan Jerkins, *New York Times* bestselling author of *This Will Be My Undoing*

"In an Afrofuturist world of barbaric debt police and an absurd heist to bring it all down, *The Payback* is a delightfully dark comedy of three coworkers turned conspirators hell-bent on revenge. This trio of Robin Hoods taking matters into their own hands out of grief and desperation will have you alternating between raucous laughs and fear for their safety. California strip malls, eighties fashion, and punk and hacker culture all combine in a tenacious cocktail of sweet justice shared by all."

—Xochitl Gonzalez, *New York Times* bestselling author of *Olga Dies Dreaming* and *Anita de Monte Laughs Last*

"Like *Ocean's Eleven* but no one's famous. *The Payback* is a love letter to the American mall, the revenge of the break room, and a laugh-cry of the gods of retail. The result is obsessive truth-telling fun, with zingers, dishy thrills, bodysuits, and a few wigs that have seen better days but are hoping to have the best one yet."

—Alexander Chee, author of *How to Write an Autobiographical Novel*

"A stylish, blazingly original take on the heist novel, *The Payback* is both a whip-smart critique of contemporary capitalism and a moving character study of the workers most often caught in its clutches."

—Grace D. Li, *New York Times* bestselling author of *Portrait of a Thief*

"Smart, sociopolitically astute, and sidesplittingly hilarious, *The Payback*'s inventive wit solidifies Kashana Cauley's place among our most entertaining social critics and novelists."

—Camille Perri, author of
The Assistants and *When Katie Met Cassidy*

ALSO BY KASHANA CAULEY

The Survivalists

The Payback

• • • • •

Kashana Cauley

ATRIA BOOKS
New York Amsterdam/Antwerp London
Toronto Sydney/Melbourne New Delhi

An Imprint of Simon & Schuster, LLC
1230 Avenue of the Americas
New York, NY 10020

First Atria Books hardcover edition July 2025

ATRIA BOOKS and colophon are trademarks of Simon & Schuster, LLC

Interior design by Jill Putorti

Manufactured in the United States of America

1 3 5 7 9 10 8 6 4 2

Library of Congress Cataloging-in-Publication Data is available.

ISBN 978-1-6680-7553-1
ISBN 978-1-6680-7555-5 (ebook)

To the student loan industry,
whose threatening phone calls made this book possible

If history shows anything, it is that there's no better way to justify relations founded on violence, to make such relations seem moral, than by reframing them in the language of debt—above all, because it immediately makes it seem that it's the victim who's doing something wrong.

—DAVID GRAEBER, *DEBT: THE FIRST 5,000 YEARS*

Payback. Revenge. I'm mad.

—JAMES BROWN, "THE PAYBACK"

Part One

The Mall

One

In the handful of minutes before our store opened, the sales day was pregnant with potential cash. Soon my boss Richard would open our front door, that plastic membrane that separated us from the rest of the mall. I'd worked myself into a nervousness that felt exciting, as if every single goose bump on my arms was the drop on a roller-coaster ride.

"Five minutes!" Richard yelled.

Audrey, Lanae, and I rushed around the store. We folded shirts. We straightened pants. We arranged sunglasses on those little racks with the bumps in them that look nothing like noses. I picked up a dust ball and put it in my pocket so I could throw it away later. At the beginning of the day, our floors had to look clean enough to lick. We went to our assigned places. Richard roamed the store. Audrey worked the cash register. Lanae took up residence in the middle. I stationed myself at the front, as the greeter. After the incident that had cost me my career, I was happy to still be allowed to be around clothes, and equally good at transmitting that happiness to everyone who walked in.

I arrived at my spot at the front of the store, right behind the plastic barrier. I took a second to look back over the store as it stood in its last moments of quiet. Before our customers would rush in and rearrange everything to their liking, as if a few thousand square feet of yellow lighting and carefully curated tables were their living room. Everything looked expensive and crisp. The folded corners of each shirt. The ironed-flat hips of a new set of jeans. The brand-new rack of five-hundred-dollar winter coats hanging in unison to signal that we'd arrived at the first week of August, just four months away from a winter that would never show up in Southern California.

Audrey folded the top shirt on a nearby table while dressed in an ironed T-shirt and jeans. I looked down at my own outfit, which didn't look as clean as Audrey's, but had more life to it. A fuchsia polo shirt with its collar popped, bro-style, and a pair of electric-blue leggings that made my legs look sharp, like pencils . . .

"It's time!" Richard said.

He walked, with a style that suited the slim, sky-blue, three-piece seventies suit he'd worn to work, to the very front right corner of the store and pressed the button that opened the door. Its plastic panels folded up like fans on their journey to the corners of the tracking bar they hung on. I took in a breath of delicious mall air. It had notes of our folded clothes, a faded disinfectant aroma I associated with the mall's interior tile hallways, a bit of fried-food smell from the Chinese place up in the third-floor food court, and the first morning note of faux butter from the movie theater right above us.

I loved mall smell. On my breaks I huffed it like glue. A five-minute commute took me to the candy store, where I could shotgun the scents of binned Oreos and Swedish Fish, their aroma dulled by plastic lids until someone opened them and sent a fire hose of sugar right up my nose. Three minutes from there stood our only pizza place, an aggressively seasonal counter that faced twelve stools and currently featured a summer picnic pizza covered in corn and tomatoes. The pizza was good. Really good! Even though there's something about explaining where you source your tomatoes from that feels like too much effort in a mall. I only treated myself to the pizza once a month. I was still working on paying off my student loans.

Half a hallway and one left turn from the pizza place lay one of those plastic horses kids can ride if an adult drops in a quarter. Sometimes, when there were no kids, I'd lean into the horse and sniff it to get a whiff of plastic, childhood dreams, and dried piss. Yes, I know, nobody's supposed to savor the aroma of pee, and I wouldn't rank it first among the smells of the world, but pee is life. It's humanity. It's the mall.

The first customer of the day walked in. A white woman of average height in a shapeless sweatshirt and jeans. Despite the bad clothes, I could tell she was a size six shirt, size eight pants, size seven-and-a-half shoe on the knife's edge between medium and wide. Size medium in belts and in coats due to a touch of width in her shoulders. She had small enough features that her sunglasses should never clear fifty-five millimeters in height from the top to the bottom of the lens, unless she needed to drown her face in a tragic sunglass accident.

"Welcome to Phoenix," I said.

She gave me the double take that everyone did if they hadn't read the store sign.

"Like the city?" she said.

"Like the bird," I said.

"Oh, phew," she said.

No, we weren't in Phoenix. Our store, which was named Phoenix, was in the middle of a mall in Glendale, California.

"Can I help you find anything today?" I said, hoping that she'd need something in the front third of the store. If she needed anything in the middle of the store, I'd have to toss her over to Lanae, and if she needed to go straight to the back, that was Audrey's turf. The only exception to this was if she wanted help, in which case I was allowed to follow her all over the store like high beams on an unlit road. I very badly wanted to get her into something more life-changing than what she was wearing. The best part of my job was leading someone's sartorial transformation into a better person, and the worst part was when a customer refused to understand that clothes could take them closer to perfection.

"No, I'm just looking," she said.

"If you need anything, let me know," I said, but she'd already taken a step or two away, into just-looking land, the territory of cowards and scoundrels. What did people expect to find if they were just looking? Coats? Shoes? The void? Nothing, that's what. I had every shirt memorized. Every pair of pants mentally indexed by size and fit. I had touched every belt in the store to understand exactly how it would wrap around a waist. If someone grabbed a pair of sunglasses that wouldn't vibe with their face, my head would cough up a full slideshow of sunglasses that would, ready for that moment when the customer leaned over to me and said, "Do these look right?" I was a trained assassin, but for clothes.

But I was also on commission. To make my 20 percent, the just-looking types would have to decide I'd helped them out the most of anyone in the store. If someone hung with me for twenty minutes and two or three fitting-room suggestions, they'd probably give the cashier my name. Especially if I walked them back there. They couldn't deny I'd helped them if I floated just beyond their elbow as they paid, with a winning smile on my face. But sometimes when people wandered away, I became just a greeter instead of a trusted assistant, or the friend you made for the duration of your time in the store. I could always see the sale slipping away in that moment, like a toilet flush.

Luckily, the next woman who walked in needed a handful of shirts for her new podcasting gig. Just because no one would ever see her shirts didn't mean she couldn't feel sublime in them. We spent a good forty-five minutes working our way through short sleeves, long sleeves, henleys, and satin blouses with darts. As Audrey rang her up, I stood at a close but not creepy distance, feeling the familiar lick of triumph that I associated with closing a sale. Some winning squads stormed the beaches at Normandy, and others left someone satisfied with six perfect tops.

Three customers later, the store settled into a dead period, and Richard went to the back room for what he called his retirees' lunch, even though he didn't expect to ever be able to afford to retire. Two hard-boiled eggs with a sprinkle of hot sauce that he kept in a corner of the break room, served at exactly ten thirty a.m. He scoffed every time we told him that we were pretty sure even retirees didn't eat lunch that early.

He left the sales floor to eat. A customer walked out, and the store was empty. I listened to the standard mix of ten thirty a.m. sounds. My own feet squeaking against the tiles as I did a moderate-sized lap around my section of the store. The tinny sound of Muzak-ed Taylor Swift playing from the speakers above my head. The gentle swish of people walking past our store to other mall destinations. The silence of no customers, which I could always hear even if music was playing. An absence of sound that had its own weird sound, like tinnitus's cousin. It swished in and out of my ears like beach waves. Lanae finished a similar lap of boredom and came over to stand with me.

"Richard look off to you?" she asked me.

"No."

"Doesn't seem a little sick or anything?"

"He always looks the same. A little stooped, hella tired, sporting the smile of the year anyway."

"I told you we don't say hella. That's a Bay Area thing."

"I like it!"

"Well, then you like being wrong."

We laughed. I loved Lanae in that way that you love people who get on your nerves an acceptable amount. For three years, between similar rounds of boredom and laughter, we'd sold people clothes together. We'd sold earth tones and the faded neons that, like the forever-lingering smell of weed smoke, were evidence of an ever-present LA stoner culture. Even our more formal clothes had a Californian air to them. We had so many dresses in fruity colors that looked perfect under the sun, like raspberry and lemon and a shade of bright orange that looked downright juicy. We had lazy oversized neon polos. Pleated skirts that rich teens wore rakishly off-kilter. Mary Janes in neutrals and brighter pastels but with a pointed toe. We sold everything from basic T-shirts to statement dresses. When I looked across the store, I always caught sight of our neons and thought of Ryan Gosling walking through all that similar-colored light in *Drive*.

Lanae, who spent her nights and weekends singing punk music with her band, shunned our bright neons and our bohemian earth tones in favor of an all-black wardrobe. That day she wore a thin black sweater with nine safety pins attached to her chest in a square formation over black stretch pants that most customers bought in neon green or sky blue. To top it all off, she'd put safety-pin-patterned barrettes in the black shag wig she always wore over her braided-down Afro. In addition to being a good work conversation partner, I liked Lanae because, clothes-wise, she had a look that didn't bore me.

Audrey took on a dull prep style to match her post behind the cash register. She looked short and severe in a rotating variety of crew-neck T-shirts and straight-leg jeans, the most boring cut in the jean kingdom. She wore only the most lifeless colors. Navy blues, pure whites, shades of tan that put me to sleep. Her hair was in its usual Black prep girl's straightened ponytail. The ballet flats she always wore had all the excitement of unbuttered toast.

Lanae always implied that Audrey was a much more fascinating person than she looked. But no matter how much Lanae hinted that Audrey had spent serious time as a hacker and might have been fired by the NSA before she'd come to sell clothes in our mall, I could only see Audrey as a person who remained fatally without style. Besides, the government didn't have style either. On school trips to DC as a kid, I remembered spotting government workers in their ill-fitting not-quite-suits, all navy "sport jackets" and tan pants just the right amount of too big to threaten to slide off their bodies in a gust of wind. If most people's sense of style was tragic, DC style was the *Titanic*.

In my first days working at Phoenix, fresh from the humiliation of getting fired off my last film set, I craved coworkers with entertaining senses of style to soothe my job transition. Even if the aftershock of getting canned led me to give up on style at work myself. I always wore one of our polos over a set of leggings, like the marooned leggings-addicted aughts New Yorker I was. It was a look I did not believe in and would never condone in other people, but also a look that didn't remind me of the high fashion I'd been addicted to before.

Besides, fashion is for the moment you're in, and as fabulous as I used to be, I couldn't imagine reporting to the mall in one of my outfits from before. If our customers saw me in a cream bodysuit, cream lace pencil skirt, pointy-toed flats, and a pillbox hat, they'd sprint down the mall hallway fast enough to slide through a just-mopped section of floor and crash into the kiosks, to suffer the tragic fate of being covered in key chains, or fake perfume, or vanilla cucumber charcoal lotion.

"Richard doesn't look a little . . . peaked to you?" Lanae said.

"He peaked forty years ago," I whispered back.

At the back of the store, Audrey rang up clothes with a look on her face that implied she'd been born without feelings. I was one of those people whose faces give away everything we're thinking, no matter how hard of a shell we attempt to put on. I never understood the Audreys of the world, those people who were good at work face.

After a whirl of customers in the early afternoon, things were dead enough that I had time to clean out the fitting rooms. Fitting rooms are the id of a clothing store. They contain multitudes. People will leave their entire lives underneath clothes they don't want to buy. I've picked up keys, pills, phones, half-eaten food, full diapers, used tampons, condoms both fresh and aged, notebooks with grocery lists long enough to feed an entire kingdom for a week, and once, a full bottle of wine. We gave its owner the usual forty-eight hours to come back for it. When that didn't happen, Lanae and I took it to our version of karaoke night, where we split it in the mall parking lot, sang disco songs at the top of our lungs, and drove home not quite drunk.

I entered a fitting room with three separate piles of forgotten clothes. One on the left side of the bench, one on the right side of the bench, and one jammed into the space between the horizontal metal bar and the wall behind it. Three different rejected lifestyles.

I picked up the pile of clothes on the right side of the bench first, which had a very pool-party-at-the-porn-shoot vibe: Pleather miniskirts. Midriff-baring T-shirts. Bodysuits in pastels that made them look like swimsuits from a distance. Neon flip-flops. A gold watch fell out of the pile. My eyes fell with it. It hit the floor face up. Patek Philippe. Hot damn. Who the hell would leave a watch this expensive in one of our fitting rooms?

I hadn't pocketed anything from a fitting room in two years. Back then, I could think of no greater thrill in life than poaching a watch, or a ring, off a fitting-room bench, and taking it to my jewelry guy, who would give me so little money for whatever I brought him that I'd feel insulted, yet not insulted enough to decline. I'd perfected the art of lifting the goods with the gentle touch that other, more boring people probably used to do something insufferable, like make soufflés. Using a pile of clothes as a shield, I could casually slip anything into my pocket that would fit. But I wasn't a swiper anymore. I'd moved past that part of my life. I didn't need someone else's watch. With commission, this job paid well enough to let me very, very slowly chip away at my student loans and live alone in a janky one-bedroom in East Hollywood. It kept me from crawling home to my insufferable mother in Brooklyn and telling her that I'd failed at life. But when I looked at its face, all I could see was money. There's something irresistible about a nice watch. Not simply its beauty, but how its worth hints at another life. A life where someone could afford to buy that kind of watch. Maybe a life with a house and one of those refinished seventies beamers everyone drove in the neighborhood next to mine and expensive, glamorous problems, instead of the everyday financial anguish that stumped me.

I eased three of the bodysuits over my arms in a way that turned them into a tiny blanket, and picked the watch up underneath them. Goodbye two consecutive years of being a better person. Hello watch. I said a silent prayer that my lowball guy would offer me at least five hundred, and looked at the watch under the sheerest bodysuit in my hands. Its golden strap had an elegance that I associated with wedding jewelry, and its gold-and-gray-accented face reminded me of those women who wore stiff wool suits and spent their Mondays flying from LA to New York to Geneva. It was such a gorgeous watch. I'd wear it in a heartbeat if I didn't need to turn it into money. I heard footsteps. I picked up all three piles of clothes, left the fitting room with the watch in my pocket, and took my haul back to Audrey, who I knew would give me shit for the size of the pile.

Audrey stood in the position she usually took on when there were no customers waiting to pay. Arms crossed, a few inches from the cash register, as if it held a magnet that kept her within a fixed radius. She and Lanae and I had all started at the job in the same month three years ago, and Lanae and I had quickly slid into hanging out. I couldn't imagine Audrey ever coming out with us. Or having friends at all. Or carrying on a conversation for more than two minutes. Or giving me eye contact that didn't feel like she was x-raying my skull. I braced myself for whatever she'd say about the enormous pile of clothes I sat on her counter.

"Richard looks kinda sick, right?" she said while grabbing a hanger for the shirt on top of the pile.

"I don't see it," I said.

We both looked across the floor, where Richard excitedly explained pants to a woman whose face said she had never experienced excitement. The woman was short. Five-two-ish. Possibly

Latina. With a hip-to-waist ratio that made pants a difficult math problem. This might have contributed to the downcast look on her face whenever Richard picked up a pair. If I was over there with her, I would have talked about high-waisted skirts or a couple of the jumpsuits that we'd all tried on and liked, despite Audrey and Lanae and Richard and I having four very different body types. But Richard was taking his customer to a different, equally pleasant place, one with wide-legged sky-blue stretchy polyester pants and a matching sleeveless, button-down shirt that tied at the waist.

"You don't see much," Audrey said, hanging the shirt on the rack behind her.

"What's that supposed to mean?" I said.

"Nothing," she said.

"I see everything. I see every customer here. Every place where clothes meet rack. Every piece of clothing. Every square of our tile floor. The dark corners of the fitting rooms. The bugs that scuttle under racks. You, me, the cosmos. It's all up here," I said, pointing to my head.

"Forget it," she said.

Audrey turned away to sort the rest of the clothes I'd handed her, dismissing me. She whipped shirts into one pile, pants into another, and accessories into a third, all in the time it might take someone to blink twice.

I went back to the front of the store, stung. Who the fuck was she? I noticed everything. What the fuck did she notice? I noticed a dust bunny slowly ambling across the floor, nine hours from its inevitable death by vacuum. I noticed the tight fit between the square horizontal end of a coatrack and its square vertical brother-in-arms. I noticed absolutely nobody coming back for the watch in my pocket. Who forgot their expensive-as-hell watch? See, a customer just walked in. Here I was, noticing the fuck out of her. Tall, blond, formal, stiffly tucked into a T-shirt and jeans boxy enough to erase any hint of personal expression.

She had a rich-enough look that she had probably meant to wander into a more upscale part of the mall, like the housewares store that sold seventy-five-dollar spatulas. Nobody needs an expensive spatula. I knew a seventy-five-dollar spatula lady when I saw one. If I had to talk to them for more than five minutes, they'd reveal that they had careers that sounded great but didn't amount to much, like art curator of their personal collection. They had family money, but they didn't want to tell you what their family did because it probably had to do with killing your family in some way. There were so many petrochemical heirs in the seventy-five-dollar spatula ranks. Sometimes they'd switch it up by being DDDs, the demure daughters of defense contractors. If they didn't watch themselves, they'd give one of us the slight pinch around the mouth that meant Audrey, Lanae, Richard, and I were a little too Black. The real question was, why did they come to the mall themselves? Didn't they have servants who did their shopping for them? Or kids who could take a second away from helping mercenaries to hit up the mall? The going theory I had was that the mall represented normality to them. A place where they could shuck the weighty responsibilities of being the heirs to killing empires to take down caramel corn.

"Jada," Richard whispered into my ear.

I jumped, since I hadn't heard him come anywhere near me.

"Honey, we have customers. Go talk to him," he said, nodding his head toward the entrance, where a lone and lost fiftyish guy had entered timidly, as if a clothing store was actually a shark pit. I looked around for the seventy-five-dollar spatula lady, who had taken advantage of all the time I'd spent ruminating about her to bypass me and wander over to Lanae. I took a moment to survey Richard as he walked away, figuring if something really looked wrong with him, I would see it with the clarity of stars in a cloudless sky. But he looked fine. Fresh, even, since his powder-blue suit made him look like he'd just stepped out of *Soul Train*.

The fiftyish guy was one of my favorite types of customers: a dad looking for something for his teenage daughter. It was almost his daughter's birthday, and he'd been sent to the mall to figure something out. Teen-girl dads were annoying because they needed all the help in the world. But I could subtly pad their purchase by claiming to be the number one expert on teenage girls, and they were usually terrified enough to believe me. I had no idea what teens liked anymore, having not been a teen for a couple of decades. I could only pretend, since the teens came into the store and wandered off to look at shirts without me. Teens have never needed anyone pushing forty to tell them what they want to buy.

Half an hour later, I sent teen-girl dad back to Audrey with a pair of slim-fit neon T-shirts and one of the maximalist backpacks that I had watched teens buy without my assistance. The backpacks had neon swirls and protruding growths that looked like unicorn horns, and looked like someone had designed them at Burning Man while high on a new psychedelic drug that made them unable to focus on anything but backpacks. Teen-girl dad looked satisfied in the mildly confused way of people who had to shop for fourteen-year-olds. But on my return to the front of the store, I saw Richard trying to pretend he wasn't slumping over one of the chest-high pants racks, a move I'd also tried, without success, when I was hungover and needed to look like I still knew how to stand upright. I ran over to him.

"Richard, do you need to sit down for a minute?" I said, gently grabbing his arm.

"No," he said, springing back all the way upright. "I was just getting to know this clothing rack. She's a real looker."

"What, are you into girls now?" I said.

"Only if they're made of metal."

We both laughed. I stared at the rack he was talking about. It was the same gunmetal gray as the rest of our racks, and it held a pack of the sort of T-shirts Richard might wear if he was going to a rave. More elegant than the rest of our shirts, with three stiff buttons below a middle-of-the-road collar that wouldn't be noteworthy if it wasn't for the colors they came in, electric blue and acid green. That was Richard, formal but fun. I wasn't quite old enough to have witnessed the rave era, just its poppier aftermath, where we thought older kids with glow sticks and hits of E were the coolest people in the world. Even if they were moving their arms like those inflatable car-wash dolls to music that sounded like synthesizers had been struck by lightning and burned to death. They looked like they were having so much fun doing it, and that was all that mattered. As much as I loved my mall, every once in a while I felt bored enough to dream of drugs, wishing I hadn't missed out on all that raver E, stayed too scared to deal with cocaine through the aughts, and eventually moved to LA to be the only person who didn't smoke weed. Any of the three felt like they might have helped with spending five days a week inside a mall.

Richard would be the dude at the rave who asked if everyone else there needed a glass of water. Yeah, he was my boss, and you can't trust bosses, but if you could, he would be number one on my list of bosses I felt good about. He asked after Audrey, Lanae, and me like we were his children. He knew when we were trying to sneak into work with fevers just to get paid, and would hold up what we called the fever hand—a hand that could take our temperature from five feet away—and tell us to go home and rest. He asked about our pets and boyfriends and petty traumas with a degree of interest I associated with therapists. On cold days he brought in his special hot chocolate, which involved melted chocolate chips and cinnamon, and we'd hustle to the break room to down it in shifts before it cooled off.

Before I could ask him if he needed a glass of water, he collapsed on the floor, taking the clothing rack with him. I dropped to the floor to ask him if he was okay, and when he didn't respond, I shook his limp shoulder and held one hand over his mouth. Fucking nothing. I didn't know CPR, so I just sat there, breathing at the speed of light. Lanae rushed over, checked for his breath, and pushed down on his chest.

"You're supposed to breathe into his mouth," said Audrey, in her usual deadpan.

I was freaking out. Why the hell wasn't she freaking out? Lanae leaned down to try to breathe into Richard's mouth, but the horror of the situation hit her, and instead of doing CPR, she screamed.

"I'll do that. You call 911," Audrey said to Lanae, who took her hands off Richard's chest and sank down next to me, in the corner for the useless. A ring of customers gathered around us to help out by staring at us in silence. Lanae called 911, and I waved away mall security, since Richard hadn't shoplifted anything and wasn't running through the food court at top speed, threatening to collide with a pack of teens. Mall security electric-scootered itself away, and the customers filed out, and then it was just the three of us with our unconscious boss. Where was 911? I laced my fingers together and squeezed until they hurt. Lanae was panting like she'd just run a marathon.

"Where is 911?" I asked Lanae.

"Sometimes they get stuck in traffic."

"You're fucking kidding, right?"

"Have you ever taken the 134?"

"Chill out, people," Audrey said, taking a break from CPR to yell at us. "We're not talking about freeways right now."

"You're not supposed to stop!" I said.

She went back to trying to get Richard to breathe. She got up after her second round of CPR and walked in a circle around a table full of polo shirts, shaking her hands like something was stuck to them. I looked down at Richard, because CPR usually worked, right? He wasn't moving, or breathing, or doing anything more normal like getting up and launching into some entertaining story about some other time he'd almost died on the sales floor. I was so ready for that! I wanted to hear all about how last time he'd keeled over in front of the sunglasses, and four pairs fell on him, and he called it his next look! Instead the paramedics showed up and tried a third round of CPR. Then they put a sheet over his head, and I couldn't move. They lifted him onto a cot and wheeled him out the store's back door. It was official. The day had turned to shit. I lay down on the floor and looked at the ceiling tile. It was still fucking tan. Maybe I'd never have to get up. Audrey walked past me, and I heard her slide the store's plastic front door shut.

I normally loved the music that played during work. It was traditional retail music, happy in its never-ending way. But right after Richard died, the store music pounded my head relentlessly in its undying upbeat loop. It was summer music. Pool-party music. Music for having a good time and buying tons of shit you didn't need. It was not death music. No one's death should ever have to be soundtracked to "Party in the USA."

Lanae came and lay down on the floor next to me. Beyond my feet, I could see flashes of normal mall behavior. Rich teenage girls languidly passing the Phoenix sign, as if the mall was their kingdom, with their arms full of bags. Not-rich teens doing what I used to do as a not-rich teen—see how long they could be with their friends in the mall without spending any money. I had fond memories of moving between sections of the fancy bookstore near my childhood apartment in Brooklyn so they didn't kick me out, and seven of us sharing a Cinnabon almost as big as our heads in the only mall we were allowed to take the train to. I still remembered the looping mall music of my teenage retail jobs, heavy on Faith Hill and Shania Twain. If you blindfolded me, cut off my tongue, and threw me into a pit, I could still sing all the words to "You're Still the One."

"They should give you a year's pay if you have to watch your boss die on the floor," Lanae said.

"Two years," I said.

"Rest of our lives."

"A big bonus on top of it. Just a waterfall of death cash."

A white woman with thousand-dollar highlights banged on the glass at the front of the store. Lanae and I eyed her, but we didn't get up.

"Have you seen my watch?" she yelled.

She was on the other side of the closed door and her voice was muffled, so her yelling and arm flailing made her look like an angry wind sock. But whether she looked stupid or not, I'd fucked up. Her watch was deep in my pocket, bumping against my hip. How could I walk over there, reach into my pocket, and hand her back her watch without her calling the cops on me? I couldn't. I sank a little more deeply into the floor, to marinate in the knowledge that I'd backslid into being someone who took watches. I always thought of the thrill of pocketing something that wasn't mine in the moment, instead of all the guilt and shame I'd be stuck with later.

"No," I yelled back.

Lanae, who knew my history, gave me a look.

Audrey came and lay down next to us.

"What the hell was that?" she said.

"You swear?" I said.

"Now that people are dying at work, I figure I can say whatever I want."

"If we still have jobs," Lanae said.

"I'll be here tomorrow," I said. "I need the money."

"All you need is Richard's store key to get in here," Audrey said. "Just go chase the paramedics down and get it out of his pocket."

"Shit," I said.

"Fuck," Lanae said.

"Damn," I said.

"Asshole," Audrey said.

We all laughed.

"Maybe it'll be all right if we never get up," I said.

"Uh-uh," Lanae said. "I have a show to play at seven."

Lanae didn't just dress punk. She lived the life. She was the lead singer of a punk band called the Donner Party. If she wasn't performing with them, she was out seeing bands with names like Soup Full of Glass and Lupus. I went with her once, because she swore I'd have a mind-blowing time, and I did. My hearing blew out in minute two, and I spent the rest of the night confusedly watching everyone else around me perform the rituals of a 1920s silent movie. They flapped their mouths and waved their hands while I waited for the end of Prohibition. The show ended, the hearing flowed back into my ears, and the speakeasies closed. Never again.

"Whatever. I'm going to have a killer time right here on the floor with Audrey," I said.

"Sorry, I'm going to meet up with my running club," Audrey said.

"You would be a runner," I said.

"What's that supposed to mean?"

"You have the vibe of a person who runs."

You know, runners. People who ate more vegetables than the rest of us in our entire lifetimes, because performance. People whose idea of a good time was getting up at five a.m. on a non-work Saturday to run in the mountains instead of lazily lying in bed until eleven to celebrate the glories of sloth. Audrey had the slim twitchiness I'd always associated with runners. An inner motor that kept them in constant motion, like a cockroach.

"See you tomorrow if we can get back in?" Lanae said.

"You know it," I said.

The other two got up and left, leaving me alone with the looping music and the cold floor. Just over my right foot was the spot where Richard quit it. This morning he walked in with his hard-boiled eggs, and now he wasn't walking anymore.

When I was in film school, I went to a Target after class once to pick up seltzer and floss, and on my way in I passed a woman lying on the floor, moaning and surrounded by paramedics. She kept yelling, "I don't want to die here!" and I looked at her with sympathy, because who the hell wants to die in a Target? But Richard had done it. He had more or less died in a Target. He had expired under fluorescent lighting, surrounded by racks of clothes, under an endless looping wave of Muzak instead of at home, or a hospital, or at least surrounded by people who didn't work for him.

I felt a new level of horror. I, too, could keel over right here, at work. I could die among clothes, surrounded by the fried-egg-roll smell of the Chinese spot in the food court so strong it could make it down here from two floors above me. For a second it didn't sound so bad. I'd rather die at the mall than in my dirty-ass apartment, awash in student loans. I couldn't imagine reconciling well enough with my toxic mother to enjoy expiring within a thousand miles of her. But thinking about dying on the store floor reminded me of my costume-designer self, the one that had bigger dreams than going back to retail, until those dreams were killed by the Incident. I didn't want to die here. Or work here forever. As much as I loved selling clothes to people, I promised myself I was not going to tap out at the mall.

Two

At home, I woke up in the middle of the night, turned over for a while, gave up on the acrobatics, and got up. Apparently watching Richard die at work didn't improve my sleep patterns. I did a lap around my apartment, which consisted of three rooms and a bathroom. A bedroom with a bed on one end and the largest closet I could afford on the other. A small room that doubled as my living and dining room in the middle, and a half row of cabinets over a stove that served as my kitchen. Every square inch of wall was covered with ripped-out pictures of Black models serving looks in everything from disco wear to modern gowns, except for the space over my bed, which had a huge *Coffy* poster, just in case Pam Grier cared to lend me toughness while I slept. I desperately wanted to keep this apartment for the privacy and because it was the only thing in my price range that had a closet big enough that it could house a sleepy Bengal tiger. But my rent was due to go up in a couple months, and my student loans were a sword swinging just above my head.

I went to my bedroom window and took in the busy three a.m. world outside. The people who worked at the night taco stand down the block were dishing out cheap al pastor tacos from a spit under a lamp between two sets of homeless encampments. Packs of teens, free for the summer, ate tacos while leaning on their cars and playing music with their windows down. The two lanes of traffic that ruled my corner of East Hollywood whooshed by with their normal nighttime hum. I took the pair of binoculars from their resting place on top of my dresser to spy on the people eating at the upscale Mexican restaurant across the street. Once upon a time, when I first landed in LA, I convinced myself that I would become an outdoorsy person beyond the act of leaving my apartment to get into my car. So I'd bought the binoculars, positive that a bird-watching future was on my horizon. But instead of watching birds, I mostly used the binoculars to try to figure out what the fancy Mexican place could possibly put in their margaritas to make them cost twenty bucks. Caviar? Liquid gold? I longed for the kind of cash that would let me waltz into that place and be a different person, a richer one, ready for the elegant experience of consuming expensive enchiladas. Just thinking about their food reminded me that I hadn't eaten anything since Richard died. My money situation seemed even darker than usual thanks to his death.

I went to the kitchen, put on the kettle for barley tea, and grabbed a bowlful of the mangoes I dried in strips out my own back window to avoid paying the shakedown grocery-store prices for the same thing. Yeah, I've stolen things on occasion, but the real hustle is grocery stores. You walk in with your wallet and they're like, nope, we're taking your car.

Three mango strips in, I remembered the watch money. There it was, in my work pants, a pack of hundreds that would briefly let me pretend I could live a different life. A slightly more cash-laden spin around the sun. My watch guy had coughed up $975, so I was feeling like an heiress who had just inherited an oil refinery. But the real treasure he gave me was a fake gold coin. He said it was worth the last twenty-five dollars of what he owed me. At first I tried to get him to give me the cash, but then I took a look at the coin and got sucked into its world. On its front it said ALL THEM HILLS ARE GOLD, and on its back it said TWENTY-FIVE DINER DOLLARS on top and GOLD LEAF DINER on the bottom. In the middle it had an address on Pico for a twenty-four-hour diner well west of me but not quite all the way to Santa Monica. The fancy Mexican restaurant across the street from me wasn't anywhere near cool enough to mint its own fake gold coins. I loved the coin, because just like the money, it spoke to a slightly different life, but one I could drive to and discover. Who went to a diner that minted its own coins?

The coin inspired me to move to my bedroom and open my closet, where I stored fifteen years' worth of fashion, from my post-college days when I thought I might become a clothing designer to all the clothes nobody else wanted on film sets. I was ready to follow this coin to its diner and temporarily become someone else, even if that other person was simply someone who went to faraway diners. I often got sick of being myself, a thirty-nine-year-old failure who worked in a mall and spent most of the rest of my time at home drying mangoes and killing ants. When I picked something out of my collection, I could go back to who

I had been then, or whoever had given me the clothes, or imagine the mysterious lives of the people who had left key parts of my wardrobe for me to find at thrift shops.

I pulled on a bobbed fuchsia wig with heavy bangs, and my favorite catsuit, one of the leftovers from after we finished filming *Catwoman: Cougar's Revenge*, a movie that came out a few years back. I'm sure a couple dozen people remember it. Catwoman robbed a few banks, but her biggest crimes were falling in love with a man with a fatal allergy to commitment, and being forty-five. Absolutely no one else wanted the catsuit, which was several thousand layers of black lace piled on top of each other from neck to ankles. It made the woman who played Catwoman look like a very dangerous and also mysteriously tight-fitting set of drapes. The movie flopped, so we couldn't auction the catsuit off or anything, and the costume shop I found it in didn't want to take it back after they discovered Catwoman had made a few cuts in the sleeves, probably as revenge for realizing the movie wasn't going to get her out of a career slump. So it was mine. I got in my car with the coin to drive to the Gold Leaf Diner.

If you drive at the right speed down a mostly commercial street, LA can become one long strip mall. Some people think that's terrible, but I don't. The strip malls give the city a deck-of-cards look. I liked gazing into those rectangles, seeing all their different combinations. At three a.m. the long strip mall was mostly closed, but there were pockets of light. I passed a pack of people eating donuts on the hood of someone's car. I passed a closed body shop with cars so broken down they looked like mouths with missing teeth. I passed a couple kissing under an old-school neon-palm-treed hotel sign from some period of LA history when they must have been trying to sell Midwesterners on the place. UTOPIA MOTEL, the neon sign gently murmured into the night. NOW WITH HBO.

I settled into the idea that I'd be driving for a while and put on music. I kept a magnet in the car I could mount my phone on for musical emergencies. The only proper three a.m. music is disco. I put on "Knights in White Satin" by Giorgio Moroder and just like that, the night became sexier. Everything now looked to be lying on top of everything else, like the strip malls and apartments had just enjoyed a good time together. Closed corner stores lay on top of closed pizza places, which got down with closed barbershops. The Moroder faded into Diana Ross, which gave way to Sister Sledge. In the middle of the night, we are all the greatest dancer.

The diner looked like an ordinary diner at first glance, with a long, rectangular parking lot oozing out its side like a half-used tube of toothpaste. But the front of its building held the same design as the front side of the coin. ALL THEM HILLS ARE GOLD, the diner glowed to the closed drugstore across the street. Both of them sat on a stretch of Pico where hills were merely an idea. The logo added mystique to an otherwise straight-from-the-diner-handbook-looking place. The history of gold was full of death and folly, but every once in a while, someone struck it rich. Nine hundred seventy-five extra dollars felt good, but man, what I wouldn't do to suddenly have a lot more money. Please, diner, give me some luck.

I didn't notice the cops until I'd already sat down in a booth. I didn't dine with cops, but after a waitress handed me a menu, it felt too late to switch booths, and if I tilted my head at the right angle, I couldn't see them. I ordered coffee and hash browns, and the waitress slid them in front of me just when I'd become bored enough to try to figure out if they were city or county cops. But their badges looked all wrong. What the fuck kind of cops wore turquoise badges? Clearly the ones who had just come back from Sedona ready to tell anyone who'd listen about some crystals they bought that would fix climate change if they held them in the right order.

The diner didn't have Cholula, but it had tiny appetizer-sized bottles of a homemade habanero hot sauce that worked on top of the ketchup and black pepper on the hash browns. The coffee tasted like good dirt. Yes, I was one of those kids who ate dirt, and at its best, dirt is layered with notes, like a good glass of wine. So I ate hash browns, and drank delicious dirt coffee, and would have ignored the cops if they weren't so damn loud.

The loudest cop had a real cop face. Some might say punchable, but not me, because I'm an upstanding member of polite society. He worked himself up into a real crimson glee as he described a single mother who had unfortunately found herself in some kind of debt, which struck me as odd, because I didn't think anyone referred to anything cops had to do with—say, traffic tickets—as debt.

"Just thousands of dollars of debt," he said, excited. "She thought the monthly minimums were a suggestion."

The other two cops laughed.

"What kind of deadbeat can't even pay the monthly minimums?" said a cop with the kind of lantern jaw and floppy white-guy hair I associated with lacrosse players. Hot white cops were such a waste.

"I know! You can negotiate them down to like, two dollars a month for the rest of your life," said a Black cop who'd wasted his gorgeous, Idris Elba–esque mug on law enforcement.

There's no need to talk when you're eating alone, but the sight of a Black cop merited an extra moment of silence. Even good-looking Black cops are the mouse that's just taking a nap in the snake's mouth.

Wait a minute. Two of the cops were hot. I took another look at the group. They all looked pretty together for cops. I mean, cops couldn't really be hot because of what they did, but these guys all had a look I wouldn't have disapproved of out of uniform. Why were they hot?

"Oh, no, I think they stopped that. You have to pay at least a hundred a month now," said Lantern Jaw.

"That's not that bad," said Black Cop.

"Yeah," said Lantern Jaw. "You can just cut your own hair."

"Or make your own coffee," said Black Cop.

"Or get another roommate," said Punchable Face.

"Or a third job," said Black Cop.

"They're just so lazy," said Lantern Jaw.

I listened to this line of conversation in total disbelief. These guys had clearly never tried to do shit like work multiple jobs, afford an apartment, and pay their loans at the same time. I was doing a hair better than that now, but I remembered darker days. I could tell them stories of my heroic, Oscar-winning performances for roles like "woman insists this pound of beans will last three weeks," and "shoe soles are for cowards." I remembered the nights where I had to travel between far-flung jobs fueled on coffee, 5-hour Energy, and the fear that I would nod off long enough to end up pancaked on the side of the 101.

"After I held one of her kitchen knives up to her throat, she suddenly remembered how to pay her debts," Lantern Jaw said.

The other two cops laughed. But I froze, with my fork-holding hand halfway up to my mouth, unable to move. They laughed and laughed and laughed, and all their laughter stabbed me in the stomach.

I, unable to listen to their conversation for a second longer, signaled for the check, handed over the coin, and headed for the door. Like a lot of diners, this one had two sets of swinging glass doors. Inside the first one I looked left and saw the vending machine I'd missed on the way in that sold commemorative diner coins like the one I'd just had in my pocket, which felt so much less intriguing now that I'd discovered that they came from a vending machine that would sell you one if you put in twenty-five dollars and had the skill to grab it with a metal claw. Nothing in those hills was gold.

I slung myself into my car and sped off. I don't know who I expected to find eating at the diner, but definitely anyone else other than a pack of cops dickish enough to laugh about threatening a single mom. And nothing wrecks the mood like listening to people talk about punishing others for their debts when you haven't paid yours off. My undergrad and film school debt followed me around like a stalker in the night. My debt eagerly anticipated this next part of my life where I might not have a job. Debts loved that shit. They could just sit there, multiply, and laugh while I tried to come up with contingency plans. As a person whose adult income tended to range from low to embarrassing, I'd paid the minimum when I could afford to and turned away whenever the loan website tried to show me how much I owed. But cops didn't seem like the kind of people who made enough money to brag about people who couldn't pay debts. Every year the news claimed they were underpaid, so they needed more money to beat people up and not solve crimes.

Either those cops were rich enough to despise us debtors like they did people who'd shoplifted a candy bar from the drugstore, or they were broke enough that they were right there in the stew with us. I made it home and went to bed, positive I'd be exhausted enough from all the driving to immediately drop off to sleep. Instead I rolled around forever, simmering in dread and a lingering sadness from Richard's death, praying I'd never fuck up enough to have to deal with those cops or their criminally ugly turquoise-ass badges ever again.

Three

Two days later, on an empty Sunday, Lanae texted me to say no one had come by to reopen Phoenix yet. I hung a left off one of the skinny streets bordering Echo Park Lake and honked when I landed in front of Lanae's building, because it made no sense to go to a funeral alone. She came bounding down in a more formal version of her daily punk wear. The same black studded jacket as always, but paired with an ankle-length, halter-topped black jersey dress that understood death could be approached in a casual yet stylish way. I'd gone with a black smoking suit from my film wardrobe days, and a matching black bowler hat with teal trim, for the barest hint of flair, since I found black boring but understood it was uncouth to loudly protest the traditional American funeral color.

"Why does Audrey live Downtown?" I said.

"Probably the closest she could get to living inside a bar," Lanae said.

"She drinks?"

"You've really got the wrong idea about her. She's not boring. In fact, she's lived a life that you probably can't imagine."

"I can imagine T-shirts and jeans," I said.

"Everybody isn't their clothes."

"That's unfortunate," I said, hanging a right on Sunset to climb one hill before the long descent into a neighborhood I couldn't stand. Downtown was evenly divided in two. The top half held Grand Central Market, fifty million bars, jewelry stores that appeared to be frozen in 1950s amber, and a set of restaurants that alternated between fast casual and the sort of hundred-dollar-per-person extravaganzas where you were supposed to coo when they set a plate in front of you that held one scallop.

The bottom half was what I called the zombie apocalypse, sometimes out loud, even though every time I said it, Lanae hit me in the shoulder. Skid Row used to be a street, but in recent years it had exploded into a whole neighborhood of people living in tents and looking past each other on the street with the faded-out stare of drugs. Lanae always gave me a lecture about luck when I mentioned that part of the neighborhood.

I very much understood that all of us are one shitty roll of the dice from pretending those camping tents they sell at sporting goods stores will hold up in the cold. But as a person who'd spent the last three years sliding down the income scale, since people could shop just as satisfyingly, if not more so, on the internet as they could in our air-conditioned box of horse-ride pee, I needed to draw a line between the zombies and me, in the hope that I would never be forced to cross it.

"Why are we giving her a ride anyway?" I said.

"Because she asked for one, and I thought it would be weird to say no, find your own fucking ride to a funeral. Also, she and I get along, even though I know you're sitting there imagining how to shoot darts into her face."

"I am not."

"You are. You have a real obvious shoot-darts-into-her-face look. You get all pinched around the mouth, and you add in a zombie stare."

"Please," I said, while thinking that, in fact, it would feel amazing to shoot darts into Audrey's face.

Fifteen minutes later, I arrived in front of Audrey's high-rise building, in the non-zombified part of Downtown. She bounded out of her building in a black sweatshirt and jeans and got into the backseat of the car.

"Is there such a thing as a funeral sweatshirt?" I said.

"It's black," Audrey said.

"Do you need a dress?" Lanae said, as the nicer one of the two of us. "We could swing back by my place and grab you something a little more formal."

"No, I'm not wearing a bicycle chain to this or whatever."

I gave Lanae a *see, she doesn't even like you* look.

Lanae gave me a wide-eyed, dipped-chin *give her a chance* look.

We drove straight to Richard's house in Highland Park. For the last three New Year's Eves, Richard had invited us to his Throwing Out the Old Year party. He decorated the place with wastebaskets, made us drink out of mason jars that he'd decorated to look like trash cans, and held a good-riddance toast at midnight.

So when I walked in, I recognized everything except the huge sign at the entrance that said REMEMBERING OUR RICHARD, with a picture of Richard in his fashion designer days of the eighties, wearing an impeccably trim forest-green double-breasted suit and matching trilby. I'd been hanging on for three days, but the sight of that perfect little hat unraveled me like a sweater. I accepted a hug from Richard's husband, who went by Christopher, never Chris. He was a linebacker of a man who reminded me of a couple of my uncles in his dedication to watching professional football after playing the high school stuff, and his bottomless appetite for red velvet cake. After saying hello, I ditched Lanae and Audrey and searched the house for a suitable place to cry.

Thank god for second-floor bathrooms. The first-floor bathroom in a house is always a party, between the person inside and the inevitable line of people waiting to get in, but getting to a second-floor bathroom requires a dedication most people just don't have to wandering all the way around someone's house. Anyone who embarks on the quest of searching for a second-floor bathroom has to steel themselves against confusing hallways, closed doors that lead to people having sex on a bed that isn't theirs, and the irrelevant questions heroes in search of alternate bathrooms sometimes have to answer, like "What are you doing up here?"

Richard's second-floor bathroom, like all the other rooms in his house, had a tasteful mix of pictures of him in clothes he'd designed himself, him and Christopher looking happier than most people ever got to be, and landscapes of places he'd been, which usually set the tone for the rest of the decorations. The second-floor bathroom was the Miami bathroom. It had lagoon-blue walls with pink trim and accents, a tiny inflatable flamingo on the side of the sink closest to the door, and a full mirror wall made up of tiny square mirrors opposite the toilet, as if the pieces of a disco ball had gotten a divorce.

I sat down on the toilet fully intending to cry, before getting distracted by the magazine rack a couple of feet away from my feet. It held a selection of retro *Ebony*s and *Jet*s, which reminded me of my mother's similar stack in the bathroom of the apartment we'd lived in when I was a kid. When I needed to escape from her yelling, I reminded myself that I also shared an apartment with her magazines, which contained a nineties paradise full of padded blazers, silk shirts, and brown lipstick. I picked up one of the *Ebony*s and plunged myself into a world as eighties as the suit Richard was pictured in downstairs on the sandwich board near the front door. Richard and I had bonded over being both former New Yorkers and real, bona fide fashion people whose career luck had sent them to sell clothes at a mall. He was a clothing designer who didn't really transition to the nineties.

"Minimalism was garbage," he told me two years ago on one of the smoke breaks I loved to take with him, even though I didn't smoke.

"All the minimalists looked like they starved themselves to the point where real colors or patterns would push them to the bottom of the ocean," I said.

"That's right, girl. Who wants to look like they walked out of the house in a piece of Saran Wrap with spaghetti straps? I wanted big, bold looks. Clothes that felt alive. Give me a big, strong shoulder that could cut glass. Everyone else wanted that too. They understood that the point was to have a look so large it made the Empire State Building feel tiny. Then minimalism hit, and people wanted to look like drowned rats. All that wet hair and flannel. Those girls looked like they were going to die in those silk dresses that were thin enough that you could count all their ribs. And those dresses had no cut! No style! You might as well have just taken the fabric off the rack and duct-taped it to them. And those men who wanted to look like they chopped logs in Seattle. There are maybe three hot lumberjacks in this world, girl, and everyone else is just playing," he said.

Richard tried to adjust. But people saw what he was still trying to do. Nobody went for his slimmed-down power suits. He showed me one once, and I had to look away so I didn't laugh. They looked like he was trying to bring tuna casserole to a steak dinner. But he got me. He understood what it was like to be exiled from the kingdom of style. When I told him about my own descent, he stifled a smile and gave me a hug. He knew the perils of a wardrobe malfunction.

Someone knocked on the door. I'd spent enough time thinking about Richard that I'd forgotten I was in a bathroom that other people might want to use. I opened the door.

"You're missing the party," Christopher said.

"I'm reading your *Ebonys*."

"You can't distract me by liking my magazines! And I love your friend."

"Lanae?"

"The one who's doing funeral casual chic."

"Audrey."

"Yes, her."

"You approve of funeral sweatshirts?"

"Yes. Richard would too. He always loved people who did their own thing at an event."

I teared up.

"C'mon. Let's go downstairs. We're having a good time. This is not one of those moments for crying. Richard didn't want his friends to remember him in a serious or dour way. No downcast faces. No eulogies. He ordered me to throw him the kind of party he'd want to be at. So he's down there in an urn that he insisted I cover with a sash in a fabric he liked, and in an hour or so we're gonna do karaoke."

"Karaoke at a . . ." I didn't want to call it a funeral, or a wake or anything, since we weren't at a church or a grave site, and nobody had put a coffin in the living room. And Richard and Christopher seemed to be running away from that kind of language. But my mother, before she lost it and started throwing plates at my head because she thought I was going to have the career she wanted, raised me as a person who went to traditional funerals, where people wore black, heard some scripture, and felt sad. What the hell were you supposed to call death parties?

"Death party," Christopher said. "This is death under the club lights. Literally, since the week before he died, he made me buy a disco ball for our kitchen."

"You're kidding."

"I'm not."

"Did he know he was going to die or something?"

"Oh, no. He just wanted a different kitchen vibe."

"Okay, I want to see that."

"And you want to do a song later."

"I'm not really a singer."

"And I'm not really a guy with a husband who just died of a heart attack. Life is full of surprises."

I laughed, and then I felt bad for laughing because he'd just said the words "heart attack," and then he laughed to tell me not to feel bad. He led me downstairs, which was packed with people dressed like a re-creation of an eighties prom. The men wore double-breasted suits in their best attempt at "Don't Be Cruel"–era Bobby Brown. The women wore straightened, teased, thin-banged hair with their shoulder-padded suits, as if they could click their heels and become Vanessa Williams. Half of me still wanted to cry about Richard's death, but the other half felt amazed that he'd successfully executed his plan to be celebrated in the style of the era when he was in his prime. I couldn't believe I'd missed the dress code that had to have been in the invite email. One of the best parts of LA was the sheer breadth of retro clothing stores at all price points. One of them would have sold me a power suit. I could have gotten me a wig. I coulda pulled off a Hilary Banks.

It hit me that if I wanted to, I could have a good time at what had truly turned out to be more of a party than a somber moment of reflection. Just looking at all the guests made me nostalgic for an era I was too young to remember.

"See, honey," Christopher said. "It's a party. Go have fun."

He patted me on the back and disappeared into the crowd. I wandered past people I didn't know in search of Lanae or Audrey and saw a karaoke machine waiting patiently for its moment in a corner. The kitchen had a spread laid out on the table that made all the other spreads I'd ever seen feel shabby and inadequate. Cheeses and charcuterie meats shared space with dried fruits and celery and carrot sticks, both overseeing dip. A fondue pot sat in one corner, surrounded by breads, strawberries, and grapes. An entire kitchen counter held funeral casseroles, brightened up by a line of candles that bordered their backs. Another kitchen counter was dedicated to desserts, where cakes and pies and brownies and cookies formed a circle of sugar that highlighted Christopher's main contribution: the red velvet cake he'd invented himself, which was such a hit that it led him to opening one of the most popular bakeries in town.

And in the center of the kitchen table, right in the middle of the action, which was exactly where he would have wanted to be, stood Richard's urn, a stately silver thing that looked like a stylish little house, with little metal windows and balconies and everything. It was draped with a mudcloth sash. I loved it. Richard, making his last fashion statement, a nod to wherever in Africa we might possibly be from. I nodded at Richard, as I would have if he were standing in front of me, took a slice of red velvet cake, and stood in front of the fondue pot for a while, dipping grapes into cheese. I didn't live on an income that gave me room for fanciness, so at parties like this I tended to hang out around the food until I was physically removed.

Someone grabbed my arm, and I looked around, relieved to find Lanae.

"Let's go out back," she said.

"Not without more food," I said.

"Fine," she said, while I grabbed a bigger paper plate to go with my red velvet cake plate and filled it with three mysterious types of casserole, bread I'd dipped in the fondue, celery and carrot sticks with their matching dip, and a small mountain of ham.

Richard and Christopher had a yard that they'd done the modern Western thing to. Tore out all the water-sucking grass and replaced it with cobblestones, rock gardens, and a water fountain with a Black angel on top spitting recycled water into the bottom dish. They'd put a bunch of mid-century modern couches and chairs everywhere, so it looked like an outdoor living room in the 1960s. Lanae and I sat on a three-person couch, me with my food, her with a look of excitement on her face, surrounded by a variety of people dressed peak Black eighties, some of whom were old enough to remember that era and some not.

"I shoulda worn a costume," Lanae said.

"I'm feeling like the only person here who isn't actually Whitney Houston," I said.

"The disco ball in the kitchen is incredible," she said.

"It didn't outshine the food," I said.

"You're so you. Also, I ran into some woman who claims to be our new boss."

"No."

"Yes," she said.

"I was kind of hoping to be our new boss," I said.

"Honey," she said. "You used to take people's jewelry. They're not promoting you. Look, they're not promoting me either, but at least they don't have me on camera doing anything shady. Besides, you want to work there forever? You want to decide that job is your life because they promoted you once?"

"They do not have me on camera. I was subtle! And it's been a long time since I lifted anything," I said, because I wasn't counting the lapse from the other day. I was back on the straight and narrow. The forward path with no distractions. Happily living in a world where my hands were never going to close around something that wasn't mine again.

"And no, I don't want to work there forever. I just wouldn't mind the money," I said.

"What is it with you and hoping for more money from a shitty job?" Lanae said.

"I like doing edgy stuff like paying rent and my student loans."

"But who gets promotions in retail? Girl, you need something else to do when you get home than think about getting promoted at a job that hasn't let us know what's going on since Richard's death."

"The store's closed. Which makes sense, since we don't have the key."

"Yeah, but we could have been making money for the last two days if someone let us in. Except for that they hate paying us," she said.

"They're not that bad about paying us," I said.

"What about that week they thought we all took off, when we didn't?"

"Okay, fine, that was terrible."

"And that time they said we couldn't sign people up for credit cards anymore after I made five hundred dollars doing it in a month."

"You weren't 'taking advantage of old ladies.' You were doing what corporate told you to," I said.

An old lady dressed as Tina Turner, from her spiky wig to her fishnets, whipped around to look at us from one bench over, probably since we'd mentioned old ladies. I gave her my retail smile, and she turned back around to the guys she was sitting with, who were doing their best Eddie Levert.

"And those old ladies were so excited to get their credit cards. Some of them would not stop telling me about how back in the day women weren't allowed to have credit. They had to put everything in their husband's name. I was doing them a favor, and then corporate decided to stop paying me for it," Lanae said.

"I'll never forget that week they talked about lowering commission rates. Who lowers commission rates?" I said.

"Thieves in suits."

"I do sometimes picture them getting all hot and bothered when they come up with some new way to make it so we might not be able to pay rent."

"This is the move that'll make them take a second job as a night driver," she said in her best boss voice.

"Or a shelf stocker," I said.

"Or someone who runs into people with their car for the insurance money."

We laughed until everyone else in the backyard stared at us.

"Anyway," I said, "who is this person so I can go in there and meet them?"

"You don't want to do that."

"I want to see what we're up against. We liked Richard, but . . ."

Lanae leaned in.

"You liked Richard," she whispered. "You're both fashion people. To me, he was just another boss. Nobody sane goes around liking their boss. We are not on the same side of the class war."

"What are you here for then?" I whispered back.

"The free food."

I cackled.

"But you're not eating anything. Fix yourself a plate. And give me a description of who I'm looking for in there," I said.

"I'm telling you not to go in there and track her down."

"But I'm gonna, so go ahead."

"I don't need to describe her. You're good at spotting people who don't blend in."

"Be right back."

I scanned the yard, where everyone looked eighties enough to take themselves out of consideration. Back in the kitchen, I polished off the food on my plate and tossed the plate itself in the garbage, so I could dedicate myself to finding this lady and not spilling anything on her. Most people have hobbies like knitting and movies and shit, but man did I love finding the person who didn't fit with the crowd. It was usually because of how they were dressed. I didn't like it when people wandered past me at work to find something without me, but at least if they wore clothes that made them into some sort of oddball, I could pleasantly imagine the contours of the rest of their oddball lives while they went on their fruitless marches around the store.

Next to the fondue, I spotted a pack of Lisa Bonets of different heights and weights but with the same telltale long, curly wig talking to a Black woman dressed like a human LinkedIn profile. When going to a remembrance for someone who used to work in fashion, never show up in a suit from Old Navy. In a room full of women wearing teased bangs and washed-out neons, I couldn't stop staring at the interloper's oversized and boxy black suit. Old Navy had great prices, and an allergy to the idea that clothes should fit, even if she'd bought the right size suit, instead of one that was at least two sizes too big. She didn't have to do that to herself.

As I pretended to be enthralled by the disco ball while subtly looking at her from across the room, I mentally did what anyone would do when looking at a suit that bad: took the shoulder pads out of her jacket, one inch of fabric out of the seams running from her shoulders to her wrists, another two inches from the seams running from her armpit to her butt, and an additional inch and a half of fabric off the bottom hem of her skirt. I also mentally threw her pantyhose into a fire pit and replaced her square-toed black block heels with a slimmer kitten heel, for sanity's sake. I couldn't solve the world's problems, but if you gave me twenty-four hours and a sewing machine, I could make those problems look better.

I searched the room for an excuse to approach her and saw a pile of plastic cups and three wine bottles sitting on the table within range. I slowly worked my way over to the wine corner and poured myself a glass of red before elegantly sliding my elbow into the circle of women so they'd have to include me in their conversation about acupuncture. Did I give a shit about acupuncture? Absolutely not. I was more of a fan of medicines that came from the doctor and the drugstore than needles in the hand. But it was time to pretend.

"Twenty-five jabs later," Lisa Bonet #1 said, "you would not believe what my left foot felt like."

An appetizer? I didn't say.

"Heaven?" Lisa Bonet #2 said.

"A lawn chair nap on a sunny day?" Lisa Bonet #3 said.

"A hostage situation?" Old Navy said.

I looked at Old Navy and smiled to emphasize how great it was that we, two people who didn't know each other, could subtly disapprove of acupuncture together, but Old Navy wasn't looking at me. Lisa Bonet #1 shot me a look, though, and I gave it right back to her. She could at least be having a more interesting conversation than this if she had to block the fondue.

"Ecstasy. Not the feeling, the pill. I wanted to hug everyone. You need needles in your foot. Trust me."

"That sounds amazing," Lisa Bonet #3 said.

They were still talking about stabbing their feet to death, but a section of my mind wandered over to the toothpicks behind the platters of bread and fruit. The second I got out of this conversation, I was going right back to that cheese.

"Yeah, I'd really like to show the right side of my back what's what," Lisa Bonet #2 said.

"I'm with you," I said to Old Navy. "I don't get it."

"You stick needles in your body, and then it feels good," Lisa Bonet #1 said.

"What's there to get?" Lisa Bonet #2 said.

"Right," I said.

The Lisa Bonets haughtily turned away from me and Old Navy, as if they were connected by the same marionette string.

"I never gravitate to the New Agey stuff people like around here. I'm bad at caring about astrology," Old Navy said.

"I'm never going to be obsessed with crystals," I said.

"Or Reiki, or any of that other healing stuff."

"Or juicing. Or eating gluten-free 'because it's healthier.'"

"All my friends have been on weird diets for months. And three days ago I met someone who burned effigies of eggplants."

"Why?"

"Apparently, eggplants are part of this group of foods that's bad for you called nightshades, and . . . wait, what am I doing? I'm sounding just like her. Forget that. I love eggplants."

"Your friend seems passionate," I said generously. "Passion is cool."

"I know what you mean, but her anti-eggplant thing was just a big bundle of nope. I'm Maria, by the way."

"I'm Jada," I said.

We shook hands.

"How do you know Richard?" I asked her.

"I didn't, really. I met him a few times at work events, but I'm here to manage Phoenix, the store he used to run, now that he, uh . . ."

"Yeah. I work there."

"Oh," she said, with the fake brightness of someone who'd come in second in a bake-off. "So we'll be seeing more of each other."

What did I do?

"Yes," I said.

"Looking forward to it," I added.

"Great!" she said. "Yay!"

She spun around and paused in the way people do when they've forgotten where they think they're going. And then she went for it. She committed to her escape. She left that kitchen like a kidnapper on the run, leaving a trail of confused Lisa Bonets in her wake. What had I done to her to make her flee?

I returned to the backyard, where Lanae had replaced her blank lap with a plate of food.

"Maybe it's just a job," I said to her.

"I think she hates me too," she said.

We both looked behind us to make sure she wasn't in earshot, but through the door I could see her having a very animated conversation with Audrey, who, as far as I knew, never made hand gestures when she talked.

"We chatted," Lanae said, "but Maria didn't seem like a crackable nut."

"Maybe Audrey's charming her with that warm, friendly deadpan of hers."

"Audrey's going off, which is weird, because the only subject I've ever gotten her onto where she couldn't shut up was running. Oh, and sometimes she'll get all animated when she talks about hacking."

"She was really a hacker?" I said.

"Secret government stuff and everything."

"I thought hackers were interesting, instead of giving off more of a *Weekend at Bernie's* vibe, if Bernie spent all his time propped up in the back of a store to re-rack clothes."

"Someday you're going to end up talking to her, and she'll blow your mind. Maybe she's doing that now. Maybe that's why Maria looks all animated."

We looked inside. Maria was flipping her hands through the air in excitement, like she was conducting a living room orchestra.

Past Maria and Audrey, the living room karaoke machine clicked on and sent a wave of feedback that made me and Lanae cover our ears in panic.

"You gonna sing?" I asked her.

"Absolutely not. I have a gig in three hours. I'm saving this voice. You?"

"Not in front of a bunch of people I don't know."

After a short speech, a guy dressed like Billy Ocean lit into "Part-Time Lover," by Stevie Wonder, as if instead of Richard, we were having a funeral for the end of Stevie Wonder's career. Before I could spend any more mental time wishing he'd picked something off *Musiquarium*, Christopher came running past us and leapt over the fence that separated his yard from his neighbors in the smoothest motion I'd ever seen by a guy in his sixties. He was followed by four of the kind of cops I'd seen at the Gold Leaf Diner, all with pristine hair. But this time, instead of turquoise badges, they wore navy uniforms with turquoise epaulets. Everyone else in the backyard with us watched Christopher's escape in horror. "Debt police," they all whispered as they scanned the yard, suddenly suspicious of everyone else. People started streaming past me, headed for the front door. What the hell were the debt police?

I looked around, but I'd lost Lanae.

I went back inside to look for her and Audrey so we could leave the party too, but I didn't see them. Fuck, where were they?

A pair of debt cops worked their way to the stairs and ascended them with the kind of urgency people show on beach vacations. I hated them. Cops always looked so chill while they wrecked your life. My head went through all twenty minutes of the only time I'd ever been pulled over for speeding. I spent them feeling like I might die at any minute, if not from the cop just shooting me for no reason, then from the stress of being pulled over while Black, all while the cop calmly rifled through my license and registration as if he was savoring a romance novel.

"These Aries moon jobs are the worst," one of the cops said.

"Beats the Mercury-in-retrograde ones," another said.

Why were they talking about astrology?

Two more cops burst through the front door, holding Christopher by one arm apiece, while a third cop followed behind them, holding a gun to Christopher's head. They led him upstairs. I heard an odd thump and felt sick. What the hell were they doing to Christopher up there? What could he possibly have done to deserve this? Since when could the police rough you up for personal debt? Wait, they loved astrology. Now I felt like I'd sized them up right in the diner. It clicked. They were turquoise cops, just back from the desert, where they'd probably been doing peyote and tripping so hard that they'd seen the righteous way: to threaten people for not paying their debts.

I reminded myself that there was nothing to be gained by trying to understand cops. Even if these new debt cops seemed more mysterious than the normal kind, they were still cops, trying to arrest a guy while he mourned his husband. For no reason, because as far as I knew, Christopher had plenty of money. The man owned a bakery famous for its two-hour-long waits. While you never know what people are up to in their darkest moments, he didn't seem like he spent the gap between mixing frosting samples buying solid-gold shirts or doing culinary school again.

Oh, right. Culinary school.

Out of nowhere, Lanae grabbed my arm.

"We gotta go," she said. "I'm not dying to meet the debt police."

We heard bangs. And thumps. It sounded like the debt police were ransacking the house in search of something.

"Where's Audrey?" I said.

Audrey suddenly appeared on my other side.

"What the fuck are the debt police?" she said.

One of the Lisa Bonets turned around.

"What do they look like?" she said. "They collect debt. Student loan debt. Nobody can afford to pay back the loans anymore, but the loan companies aren't taking that for an answer."

Well, fuck. And here I thought I'd have to commit some other act to hear from the debt cops. A crime on top of my debt. But somebody had just gone ahead and created new cops who could get me for what I'd already done.

"Come on," Lanae said, hustling us both to the front door.

The three of us sprinted down the block to my car. Only after I'd started it and drove off did I dare to look back to see if the debt cops had decided to follow us, but they hadn't. I flew to the 110 on the way Downtown, to drop Audrey off first.

"I thought Christopher was too old to have student loans," Lanae said.

"No, he went to culinary school," I said. "And Richard went to fashion school back in the day. They probably both have debt."

"They changed the law so that you can inherit your dead relatives' debt too," Audrey said. "When my dad died, they assigned me his debt."

"You're kidding," Lanae said.

"I tried to see if I could get out of it, but guess what? You can't. They're going to give you as much debt as they feel like, and get that money back no matter what it takes," Audrey said.

"So they invented cops to get it back," I said.

"Why the fuck would we need debt police? The regular cops aren't enough? The student loan companies aren't mean enough? I missed a payment once and got like, eight phone calls," Lanae said.

Lanae had debt too. It was one of the things we'd bonded over in our early days at the job. We were the kind of people who took jobs without any real hope of paying it back. She'd studied classical violin until she'd learned her real tastes leaned toward punk, and if there was one thing the student loan industry punished you for, it was changing your mind in college. Like me, she'd been first-generation college in an era where college was supposed to be the answer to all the questions we could have possibly asked ourselves at age eighteen. The thing about being first-generation college was that no one we knew had any idea what the hell we were supposed to be doing there other than taking some classes and hoping they added up to a grand theory of our lives. So she'd spent six years paying a college to figure herself out, resulting in a number she owed that, due to its amount and the interest rate she'd got on it, would follow her around, like a puppy in search of attention, for the rest of her life.

I didn't make enough money to pay off my loans, but I made just the right amount to hit the minimum most months and be reminded that I still had decades of payments to make. Other, more fortunate people might spend thirty years paying off a mortgage, but so far I'd spent the fourteen years after film school watching the interest rate on my loans balloon and the final payment date get pushed back to some awful year that I couldn't be sure would predate the heat death of the planet.

I got off the freeway and descended into the nicer part of Downtown, in the darkness between the high-rises. Downtown was always kind of dead on the weekends, but the people who were still walking around between all the restaurants looked happy, like they hadn't just escaped a police raid. I felt angry just looking at their untroubled faces.

"So why do the debt cops ransack your house when they can just drain your accounts?" I said. "Are they looking for couch-cushion money?"

"I bet Christopher has a piggy bank full of quarters," Audrey said.

"Honey, you know cops have always loved our people," Lanae said as I pulled up to Audrey's building. "They found another way to show they care."

"How deep is it really?" Audrey said, opening her door. "They're clearly there to threaten people. They're cops. They're not invading your house to find themselves."

She shut the door and walked off.

I headed west and north out of Downtown to drop off Lanae.

"I'm just annoyed that I have to think about another kind of cop," I said to Lanae.

"They haven't gotten all the Black people yet," she said. "And they won't. They just like to keep us afraid. I can't live my life in fear of them, and you're not going to either."

Four

Audrey texted Lanae to let us know we could go back to work, and Lanae texted me, so on Monday I showed up at the mall. I walked in with gratitude, as if I were being reunited with an old friend instead of a job I hadn't worked in three days. Inside, I took a deep breath. Caramel corn. Dusty tile floor. Traces of disinfectant. Cinnamon rolls. Two floors above me, in the center of the darkened food court, waiting for its ten a.m. lights, sat Cinna Mon, the vaguely Jamaican-themed cinnamon roll place. How Jamaican? I think they had a curry cinnamon roll they made if you asked for one, but nobody ever did, so the Jamaican-ness was confined to the picture of the Rasta guy holding a tray of cinnamon rolls on the sign.

Upstairs, the cinnamon roll lady, judging by the smell, had just taken the day's first batch out of the oven and put in the second. She'd frost the first set with a thick cream cheese icing and put it out under heat lamps to cool to a perfect level of lukewarm while the second batch kicked even more pastry smell into the air.

People say a good restaurant has terroir, and so does a mall. Its cinnamon rolls don't taste the same in an airport, or at home. They taste right in the mall. That cream cheese icing just doesn't melt into that brown sugar and cinnamon interior in quite the same way at the park, or in a car, or on the downward edge of a ski slope I couldn't afford to go to, I'm sure. Just like trying on a sweater doesn't feel the same under light that isn't that particular shade of yellow that malls believe in, somewhere between an egg yolk and Chernobyl after the blast.

I walked through the darkened mall on my way to work, while around me, other employees of other stores bent down to the floor to unlock them from the front and enter to prepare for a day like mine, which would be spent folding and hanging and cleaning and putting clothes back. Or volleyballs, or bottles of hand soap, or athletic shoes. Together we picked up the sales-floor garbage we hadn't seen last night before our stores closed. We took swift, confident walks around our selling areas to confirm that everything in them looked as neat as the place settings at a royal wedding. We took deep breaths, and opened our front doors, and began the first day of the rest of our selling lives.

The only thing wrong with the vibe was Maria, who'd reported to work in what might have been the exact same black suit she'd worn to Richard's remembrance. She'd left her hair curled for the party, but here she'd gone for that chemically straightened helmet I associated with clueless Black women of my mother's generation. They always thought straight hair made them fit into white culture better when, if anything, relaxers made us look Blacker than ever, but with more scalp wounds and cancer. When Maria looked at me with disdain, I patted the back of my timeless tiny Afro and drew upon the strength of all my ancestors who had sported what naturally grew out of their heads to get me through the moment.

"Girls," Maria said.

Audrey and Lanae stepped out from wherever they'd been hiding to stand next to me.

"I know we're all sorry about Richard, but we have to move on and focus on sales, which haven't been great lately," she said.

We all nodded very calmly, even if, in my case, the inside of my head was screaming at her to fuck off. Mourning was not a missile sent to attack our sales. It was a state of mind that I was going to carry with me for more than a couple of days. What was the point of her bringing up that Richard died if she only wanted to note that she didn't care? How was insulting his death supposed to motivate me to sell more clothes?

There are so many ways a retail job can make you feel like shit. I'd always found what we sold to be appealing enough to enjoy working at Phoenix, but man. What about everything else? What about the half hour folding clothes before and the half hour cleaning everything in the store after? What about all the fitting-room body fluids and half-eaten food and used tissues, swarming with germs? Sometimes after an entire day of standing up, my feet felt like Hot Pockets that hurt and my lower back gave off signs that it might have been electrocuted somewhere in the middle of my shift. To all these other insults, Maria added her speech about how showing visible signs of mourning my boss, who was also my friend, was a sign of weakness that would clearly send our customers fleeing to the safety of other, more stoic corners of the mall, untouched by death. I loved my job! I really did! But every six weeks or so it started to feel like being trapped in a cage with a mechanical horse and a lifetime's worth of Dippin' Dots.

Maria droned on about really, really, really making sure people bought clothes, as if we didn't do that every day already. I turned my head the exact amount I could while still pretending that I was paying 100 percent attention to her bullshit and saw Richard everywhere. He was up near the front folding pants in that way that only he could. Three quick motions. Flip, flip, flip, and the pants would be ready for a table or possibly a war, since he was the only person who could put a fold in pants sharp enough to stab your forehead. He was listening to complaints about my nonexistent love life over a hard-boiled egg in the back. He was putting the egg down on its aluminum foil bed to do hysterical imitations of the shitty guys I gave up on. Figuring out how to pay all my bills took up too much time to have anything left over for men who wished I was a little nicer or richer or hotter. He was transforming someone in a shapeless outfit into a queen of the mall with two new shirts and a gleam in his eye. He was whispering, "You're better than this" in my ear like I could go out and get another film wardrobe job after the Incident.

"Jada, are you listening?" Maria said.

"Of course," I said.

"We need to get our sales up by twenty percent in a month."

I always imagined corporate sitting around in suits as shitty as Maria's in a high-rise in some city as dull as they were, rolling a pair of dice to come up with a sales number to scare us with. A year ago I'd almost had a heart attack when Richard came back from a meeting with them and told us they said we had to get our sales up by 43 percent by the end of the quarter. How the fuck does anyone sell 43 percent more clothing in three months? I pictured us leaving the mall and going door-to-door like knife salesmen in old movies, visiting house after house to hype up different fabrics and cuts until we'd given everyone a bloody, insatiable demand for new clothes. Did we sell 43 percent more clothing in three months? No. Did the store go under? Nope.

Our mall sat in the middle of a suburb with a grand tradition of going to the mall, and people really still did it, unlike in plenty of other suburbs, where declining incomes and mall disinterest had metastasized into empty buildings with matching parking-lot voids. But we weren't necessary. I loved trying on clothes in person under the lights to see if I was making the proper statement, but even I understood the allure of letting life come to your doorstep. If people didn't want to physically show up at the mall, we couldn't make them. But never trying on clothes in public ever again? That was a form of death. It's not about the bad lighting, or the fear that someone will see you in a swimsuit. It's about the thrill of becoming a new person while surrounded by other people who are equally in awe of your transformation.

"So today's goal is to get one more item into everyone's hands," Maria said. "Are you girls ready?"

"We're ready," we said.

There are no new strategies in retail. All the bosses can ever say is "get people to buy more stuff." We tried everything. Coupons. Sales. Surprise sales. Holiday sales. New merch. Old, clearanced merch. New words for clearanced merch that would make it even clearer that it was on sale. "Welcome to the basement." "Prices so low your mom thinks they're a scandal." "Estate sale," like a bunch of polos and wide-legged jeans suddenly constituted an estate. Sales pegged to stranger and stranger times of year. "Post-holiday sale." "Pre-Easter sale." "Take 20 percent off our clothes for National Donut Day." Stronger compliments. "Those jeans make your hair look alive." Comparing them to celebrities they definitely didn't look like in that dress. Every day I had to swear that people were trying on shirts that would change their lives. Shoes that would instantly transport them to the beach or the mountains or that trendy sushi place where they gave everyone who served a look better fish.

Maria had turned today into a one-extra-thing day. We'd had those before, and they worked just as badly as everything else. The lovely part of trying to sneak just one more thing into everyone's hands is that it's more degrading than most of the other failed strategies. Everyone knows if they meant to grab one white shirt and definitely not two, so if you, say, sneak that second white shirt into their stack they will give you the evil eye, which will not get you a two-shirt sale. It runs the risk of getting you a zero-shirt sale. People are also immune to checkout sunglasses, checkout nail polish, checkout scrunchies, and anything else little and under ten bucks that we put at checkout right in front of their not-at-all-hungry little hands. So as Maria opened the door that separated our store from the rest of the mall, I prepared myself for a day of debasement.

A few minutes later, I greeted my first customer. A Black woman. Five-five, slim, flat-chested in that way that means shirt darts would make her look like a deflated balloon whose Prozac hadn't kicked in yet. A size 26 in pants, a size eight wide in shoes. Her look was that outdoorsy business casual that I always thought of as white water rafting in the office. Medium-wash tapered jeans. A collared white button-down shirt that would be just as at home under a suit as inside a country club. One of those puffy vests that looked like she'd grabbed it out of the emergency bag on an airplane and dyed it a shade of dark brown that told the world she had the boring taste of an undercover international spy. It's awful to sigh at a new customer. I'm a better person and saleswoman than that, so I didn't, but I really, really wanted to, because she didn't belong in our store. Our entire deal was louder versions of what she had on. She didn't look like someone who would bother stooping to buy what we sold, much less buying that extra thing that would get me in Maria's good graces. But here she was, in front of me, which meant I was contractually required to be happy.

"Welcome to Phoenix," I said. "What can I help you look for?"

Customers should never be asked a yes-or-no question. Any question fired at them has to have one of those indeterminate endings that makes the customer have to spit out at least one, maybe three full sentences as to why they'd like you to go away so they can shop in peace. Inferior versions of this question, like "Is there anything you're looking for today?" let them escape you with a simple "no," leaving you bereft, unlikely to make a commission, and sadly drifting along the sales floor like a tumbleweed in fifteen-mile-an-hour winds.

My customer paused for a second, giving me just enough time to wonder if she was one of those people who planned to escape me the hard-edged way, by saying, "Nothing," so I could have that tumbleweed feeling with a side of being spiritually slapped in the face.

But then she brightened in that way that meant we might spend an hour together.

"I think my look is a little dull," she said.

That's right, girl.

"And I came in to pick out a couple of lively outfits for some events I have coming up."

I could not cheer, or give her a high five, so I adjusted my smile to something socially acceptable instead of the total giddiness that threatened to bubble up and wreck the moment. At work there was no better feeling in the world than when the universe dropped someone on me who wanted to spend real money.

"What kind of events?" I said.

"A friend's wedding, and an awards ceremony."

"How exciting," I said, a phrase I used for everything except funerals. "I'm going to grab a few things for you to try."

I took her on the store tour. We moved smoothly from rack to rack in the way I imagined gazelles would, if gazelles shopped in malls. I handed her a quality selection of dresses from all over the fanciness scale. Two simple pastel high-necked sleeveless shifts with tasteful tea-length hems in turquoise and periwinkle. A single-shouldered polyester statement in sunset orange with an asymmetrical hem that slashed from just below to just above the knee. A pair of lace dresses, one a short-sleeved A-line mini in a warm red, and the other a bright yellow maximalist number with a fitted, square-necked bodice and a voluminous pegged skirt that fell just above the ankle. I set her up in a fitting room with two pairs of sample two-inch heels in her size, one white, one black, both pointy-toed. Time to wait.

From my spot close enough to her fitting room to be right there when she opened the door but far enough away not to be creepy, I surveyed the store. "Sicko Mode" sounded extra soothing in Muzak because I was about to make myself some money, even though they bleeped a quarter of it out. I noted a tissue on the floor, the fallen comrade of the quarters and lint in someone's pocket, and picked it up to throw it out later. Lanae huddled with another customer across the store (short, Asian, twenty-five-inch waist, a size four on top and a six on the bottom, six-and-a-half shoe), who enthusiastically accepted four pairs of wide-legged polyester pants to try on. The pants said she worked one of those jobs where people tried to come off as relaxed and artistic. For Lanae's sake, I hoped the woman would buy two pairs of pants and then accept a third, at the last minute, at the cash register, to make Maria happy. This get-your-customer-to-buy-one-more-thing thing will have you cheering for freak accidents. Cyclones. Hurricanes. A barrette to accidentally fall into someone's hand within ten feet of checkout so they can suddenly decide they can't live without it so you don't lose your fucking job.

My customer came out in the first dress, the periwinkle shift.

"Very Jackie Kennedy," I said.

She nodded approvingly at her reflection and shut the door again. Two-to-one odds she'd buy it, in my opinion. She had that buttoned-up vibe that said she'd dreamed of being compared to

Jackie Kennedy. The practical rent-and-student-loan-paying side of me hoped she'd suddenly decide she had three or even four events instead of two, or that one of these events would require all its guests to make multiple costume changes. If she bought all five dresses, it would make my week. But the idealistic side of me found the Jackie Kennedy thing boring. We are not all meant to look like we just stepped off a boat in Capri, or Nice, or Martha's Vineyard. Especially when we're Black. I had flashier, more colorful ideas of sartorial excellence. I was there to slide my customers toward what they wanted, but if I could have dressed all of them, they would have looks that turned anyone who saw them to stone.

People should get dressed in the morning to be remembered at night. I love a good six-inch heel or a shoulder sharp enough to slice an apple. I'm tall and thin, and when I was a kid I found tall thinness dull, but in adulthood I realized a tall, thin body could be a canvas for more interesting ideas. In college everyone else put up posters of bands or cheesy sayings or pictures of their hometowns, and I'd covered the only wall I could lay claim to with an enormous poster of Grace Jones's album cover for *Slave to the Rhythm* to freak out white people with the title and pretty much everyone with the image itself. It had her mouth and flattop stretched a good three times longer than mouths or flattops actually go.

But it was never just about posters. There were only three looks in my upstate New York college town. Athleisure, preferably dedicated to our middling football team. Ski parkas, so the richer kids on campus could pretend to give off an air that said they'd been skiing in Utah instead of the Poconos. And whatever people in 2002 thought hippies wore in the sixties. I spent one semester trying to choose between the predominant looks, and the other seven building better ideas after class, sometimes into the night, with a sewing machine I'd found at a thrift shop. Everyone else was wearing track pants and football team sweatshirts, and I was sewing layers of tulle into one-shouldered dresses to give off a laid-back prom-on-Tuesday-afternoon vibe. I was already a Black freak in a practical rust belt town where the other Black kids were almost all normies. I leaned into that freakiness and made it mine. I became myself. A person with a look. Everyone should have a look. A strong look. A look that told other people that they were not to be fucked with. Or simply a look that wouldn't work on someone else.

My customer came out in the bright orange one-shoulder asymmetrical dress looking like she'd struck gold. The right look relaxes not just the customer, but anyone who happens to lay eyes on her. At the edge of my vision, I saw two other customers glance at her and relax, their bodies going a tiny bit slack in celebration.

"That's good," I said to my customer.

"Yeah," she said, already turning back to the mirror, which was always a great sign. I want all of them to be more in love with the mirror than me. If they're looking for my approval, they haven't given it to themselves. She shut the door, and, as usual, I began my silent cheer for the two edgiest dresses. The orange asymmetrical dress, which looked like a winner, and the yellow maximalist pegged number.

Lanae gave me a look, walked over to within earshot, and pretended to straighten a rack.

"Maria's pissed," she whispered.

"Because we're not loading people down with barrettes they don't want?"

"It's deeper than that. She came into the break room when I was grabbing a cup of coffee. She thinks we fold wrong."

I groaned. Folding was the tiniest, pickiest thing a boss could yell at a retail worker for. We could whip out the little plastic folding devices that looked like cutting boards for shirts. We could press our shirt corners into points until they looked as crisp as the edges of a fresh top sheet. We could even iron a set of shirts in the back room. No matter what we did, a manager with nothing to do could still decide that our shirts looked sad, or limp, or depressed.

"And that we leave all the stuff customers put on the floor too long," Lanae said.

"Gotta grab that gum the second someone leaves it in a pants pocket," I said.

"I've been practicing my diving technique so I can attack those used tissues they drop like a shark that smells food."

"Ladies," Maria said from behind us.

We turned around.

"I'm sure you have better things to do than talk. Lanae, come with me. There are some things you can straighten up in the back room."

We looked at each other in horror. There were other customers on the floor who might need help. And the second anyone put themselves in back, even more people could show up, decide there weren't enough people working, and leave, taking our beautiful commissions with them. Also, Lanae was being led into hell, a land of heat, dust, and shelves so high she'd risk death by collapsing ladder every time she climbed up in search of an extra shirt.

"And Jada, I need to talk to you," Maria said.

"I'm with a customer."

"After that, then."

"Okay."

Maria walked away. My breathing tightened up. My wait for the customer to try on the last real contender turned ominous. Waiting for a customer to come out of a fitting room always took forever, but now the music slowed. The silence between songs felt louder. I looked at a rack of black pants and dust rose off them to hypnotize me with its lazy drift through air. Audrey was ringing up a customer, and Lanae was facing her ominous back room fate, but I was stuck in the stasis between boredom and dread.

My customer came out in the short-sleeved red lace dress, which was a no. It turned her body into tomato soup and her face the sad crouton stuck at the bottom of the bowl. She stepped out in it, caught my eye, grimaced, and shut the door before we could say anything to each other. Her straight-up hating a dress added a second layer of dread, on top of the looming threat of Maria. Sometimes, when a customer hated one of the things I handed them, it threw off their mission too much, and they wouldn't leave the store with anything. In the future, if malls still existed then, I imagined they would replace all of us human retail workers with robots who would anticipate moods, like a customer's lack of confidence due to trying on one bad item of clothing, and spray something comforting like lilac-petal air into the fitting room to get them back on track and buying.

I looked to the back of the store, hoping to see Maria in an attempt to read her face and figure out what I might be in for, but only spotted Audrey behind the cash register, folding clothes and looking emotionless, as always. Since no boss in the history of bosses ever wanted to talk to an employee for good reasons, I spent the rest of my time waiting on my customer to try on the last dress going over everything I could have possibly done wrong. I thought my sales were fine, but maybe Maria had found something to pick at. Maybe I could sell more pants, or shirts, or belts. Mostly I wondered if I should have tried to be more like Audrey, who seemed to float unnoticed in the store, happy enough in this new kingdom run by a woman in a shitty rumpled suit.

Someone came to pay, and Audrey rang up their shirt and jeans with the mild pleasure she displayed during the more active part of her job. When that customer left, she flipped back to her default dull self as neatly as a window blind snapping shut. I loved handing people armfuls of clothes that might make them a better version of themselves, but at my core I knew working retail wasn't anything to ever be excited about. It was just the closest I could get to my old job. If I couldn't dress people in clothes that mattered, I could at least make money selling clothes that didn't.

My customer came out in the last dress, the yellow pegged-skirt one, all smiles in the way that people smile when they've hit their version of the lottery. She was greeted with the silence that happens when everyone else in sight also thinks you're in the right dress.

"That's fantastic," I said.

Behind me, a woman clapped.

"You have to get it," Lanae said, from across the store.

"It's amazing," Audrey said loudly from the cash register.

"I want this," the customer said, before popping back into her fitting room to change.

Under normal circumstances, I would have allowed myself to mentally celebrate a job well done, but next came the hardest part. The quest to find one more thing I could come extremely close to jamming into her hand at the cash register, to get that add-on sale. I had to go into my chat with Maria with the satisfaction of a job well done. And I loved a challenge. Nothing was as challenging as an add-on sale. While my customer made the rustling sounds that said she'd be out soon, I cased the store, looking for the perfect finishing touch. I flipped past the jeans, the T-shirts, the skirts. I lingered over the smaller stuff near the cash register but thought I could go bigger than ponytail holders. I never understood why we put phone cases there, as if someone would suddenly discover theirs was cracked while they waited in line to pay. Halfway between the cash register and the front of the store sat a table full of cardigans. I had a practically religious objection to cardigans in August in LA, but so many of the people who lived here thought a seventy-degree night was the Arctic. My customer had a yellow-toned warmth in her skin, so I picked up a periwinkle cardigan with pearl buttons that would set off the colors of both dresses and her complexion, and waited for the right moment.

She came out of the fitting room with the yellow maximalist number and the one-shouldered orange dress in hand. I hid the cardigan behind my back, since if I got it to her when she was standing too far away from the cash register, it wouldn't count as an add-on. Maria had to see me do it. When the customer hit the right spot, I started the fastest walk I could toward where she waited in line while pretending to remain calm, cardigan in hand, ready for that moment of victory when I handed her the perfect matching piece.

I only made it three-quarters of the way to the spot I needed to get to on the sales floor before I slipped on something. My feet went under me, and that violent motion sent the cardigan flying through the air. I belly flopped onto the sales floor, where everything went purple and dull from the hit to my stomach, but I remembered to look up in time to see the cardigan slide seamlessly into her arm as she reached the front of the checkout line, under both Audrey's and Maria's watchful eyes. My customer picked up the cardigan with the hand that wasn't holding her dresses, looked it over, and put it on top of her pile. Success!

"I don't see the woman who helped me," the customer said, "but her name was Jada."

I'm right here, I didn't yell, since there's nothing like a good belly flop onto a linoleum floor to make you forget what the hell breathing even was, much less how to talk to anyone. But I did it. I sold her an add-on. I fucking ruled.

Maria came over to help me up from the floor.

"Let's go to the back room," she said.

Two minutes later, we were watching security footage. There I was, sliding the watch out from underneath the pile of clothes. There I stood, looking directly up at the security camera like a rube while I very obviously tried to hide the watch under my pile of shirts and pants. There I went, out of the fitting room, facially convinced that I was the slickest thief on earth. Maria looked at me. I suffered my way through the form of death that is called getting caught.

"We'll mail your last check to the address we have on file," Maria said.

She left to go back to the sales floor. I walked to my break-room locker, grabbed my purse, and slunk out of the store, carefully avoiding Lanae's and Audrey's eyes. I know walks of shame are for mornings after hooking up with the wrong guy, staging an escape, and carrying heels down the sidewalk on the way back home, covered in mascara that looks like football eye black in the judgmental light of day. But there's nothing like a walk of shame through a mall, which combines that same sense of humiliation with an eternal view of ridiculous shit for sale.

My stomach still ached from the belly flop as I turned into the mall hallway and headed to my car. Fuck you, lotion sample girl. Who the fuck wants their hands to smell like blueberry pine-scented vanilla anyway? What kind of fucking smell is that? That's a fucked-up donut somebody left in the woods! The caramel corn smelled cloying enough to knock me out and hide me in someone's basement. The sports store tempted me for reasons I didn't understand, until it came to me: it would be fun to hit Maria over the head with one of the skis in the window. She would crash to the floor, just like I had, but since this time it wouldn't be me falling down, I could laugh. I nodded and smiled at mall workers who I'd known for three years, but my rage wouldn't let me hear whatever the hell they were saying to me.

My anger lit the inside of my head on fire. Who the fuck had sold me out? Lanae wouldn't. Audrey might. Was this

Richard's last present to me? Had he somehow made a supercut of store footage of me making questionable decisions and sat on it, waiting for the right moment to spring it on me while he pretended to like me to my face? Or was I so fucking obvious that whoever looked over the security tapes just couldn't resist turning me in?

Right before I got to the mall entrance that would take me to my car, I spotted one of those mechanical horses for children that always smelled like pee, and I knew what to do. I ran right up to it and punched it in the side. Wow, that hurt. But I did it again. And again. And again. My hands felt like they were coming apart at their seams. It was a beautiful feeling. A feeling I deserved, since I was a crook.

I didn't even notice the mall security guy roll up to me on his electric scooter until he was there, gamely sticking a hand between me and my plastic enemy. I fled his pity, found my car, and spent the entire drive home dreaming about smashing it into everything I passed. In the state I was in, I could destroy everything I saw. And then I got home, checked the mail, and saw that I was the one who would be destroyed.

"Dear borrower," the envelope in my hand said. "As of three weeks ago, the interest rate on your student loans has been increased by two percentage points."

Two percentage points. Thousands of dollars that I could not fucking afford over the lifetime of the loan. A number that posed even more of a threat now that I didn't have a job. I hated how the term was "lifetime of the loan," like that fucking loan had just as much of a right to live as I did. I closed my eyes and saw the debt police, in their turquoise epaulets, asking me at gunpoint how I'd dared to fall behind on my payments. Why had I spent my precious time at the mall punching the shit out of that indifferent mechanical horse, when I could have done the smart thing? Gone up to the food court, taken the hidden stairway up to the roof, and jumped off it for the glory of killing myself amid the smells of a dozen different kinds of fried food.

Part Two

The Debt Police

Five

Six months had passed since I got fired. All around LA, my neighbors, I was sure, were gleefully exchanging baskets of February lemons from their trees, or selling clothes tired from ten years of washing at swap meets. Or shotgunning tacos. Or doing whatever other manic pixie Angeleno stuff they were into, while I prepared to eat two pounds of shrimp on camera as loudly as possible for money. Shrimp didn't annoy me as much as sucking on mussels on camera, or trying to make vegetables sexy to people who really needed eating noises in order to get off. No matter how hard I tried, I couldn't wring enough sound out of a cucumber to get people to pay me.

I wandered over to my sink, full colander in hand, camera and sound ready to go, to rinse two pounds of shrimp. On the counter next to the sink I had some parsley, a couple tablespoons of butter, some olive oil, and a whole chopped head of garlic. I'd tried downing unseasoned food for efficiency, but that's no way to live.

Yeah, there weren't any other jobs in retail. I went through three interviews at boutiques that hated the way I folded shirts, four interviews at boutiques that loved me right up until the magical moment when they had to check my references, and the silence of another fifty clothing stores that never bothered responding to my applications. I didn't have restaurant experience, and going around to restaurants insisting that I could cure that by working for them didn't pan out. I drove for pay for exactly two weeks until some dude I picked up from the airport pulled a knife on me. The sex hotlines all said my voice was too nasal, and no one wanted to pay to see my feet. Honestly, I wouldn't pay to see my feet either. The second toe on my right foot is really long, and the third toe is really short, giving the whole foot the vibe of an antenna split in half. I thought thirsty internet guys would shell out cash to whack off to anything, and was disappointed to learn that my right foot represented their Maginot Line. So here I was, in my apartment, eating food on camera in the hope that internet people, mostly guys, according to their screen names and Cash App handles, would pay my rent.

I usually pre-taped all my eating, but today I'd offered my fans an extra-special treat: a live show. I turned my mic on. I pressed record on the camera, slowly washed each shrimp, and put it back in the colander. Next, I moved to the stovetop and put in the butter, olive oil, and garlic. Next the parsley, and last the shrimp. I always jacked my mic up to the most sensitive setting, so even cooking noises would have a whisper vibe to them. After a couple of minutes, I put the cooked shrimp in a second bowl, moved it over to the table I kept in a corner of the kitchen to eat, and sat it down next to the bowl I'd put out for the tails. I ate slowly, to emphasize that pop shrimp make on the first bite. I put each tail down firmly in the tail bowl to create another source of noise, and licked each shrimp at least twice before putting it in my mouth. I made most of my bank off amplified licking sounds. And anything crunchy. Never underestimate the earning power of crunch.

Am I the world's best ASMR shrimp licker? Absolutely not. I'm really more of a fiftieth-percentile on-camera eater.

Eating on camera paid my rent, but not enough to even think about hitting up the loans. After I missed the first payment, the loan people sent me weekly letters. Sometimes they called me twice a week just to say hi, as if I were a member of a generation that picked up the phone. To at least temporarily throw the debt police off, I put through an official-but-fake USPS change of address. The thrill of receiving bad clothing catalogs and credit card offers that would leave me even more financially screwed hadn't lasted. No one had the good sense to mail me cash. The only people who bothered blessing me with money were filling up the comments section of the video as I ate, saying shit like *Girl, I've got a shrimp you can lick.*

But the worst part of the job was structuring all my other eating around the enormous amounts of food that I had to eat on camera. I'd started out with regular-sized meals, but the fans wanted more. At first I thought they wanted me to do more whispering, but I slowly caught on to the fact that they literally wanted me to eat more food. So I ended up eating one meal on the taping days of Tuesdays, Wednesdays, and Fridays and three the rest of the time. My relationship to food became a little odd. I'd go grocery shopping, stare at food, close my eyes, and imagine what it would sound like to eat. Graham crackers whispered and crackled into my ear. Almonds snapped. Celery sticks crunched. The entire grocery store came alive with the eating noises all the food would make under the force of my recording setup.

Was this a life? Not really. In addition to the torture of noisy food daydreams, I'd gotten sick of my apartment, which I basically never left. Sometimes I ached for a job that wouldn't make me imagine the amplified, rubbery sounds of me running my teeth down an eggplant. On the other hand, no one was leaning over and aiming their stale breath at me while telling me that I had to refold a pair of pants. So I ate shrimp. And mussels. And surf clams, because the effort to pull them out of their shells gave me a very satisfying snap to work with. I trawled the seafood aisle at the store with the passion of a detective sure he was five minutes away from solving that murder.

After I finished the last shrimp, I did what I thought of as my specialty. I licked the bowl. Slowly, in long stripes, taking all that butter and garlic into my mouth. I knew they would hear it as one long groan. They sent me their applause emojis, and their *ahhhhhs*. I shut off the camera when I finished and went to lie down on my bed in the fetal position to take a minute after a long day at work. Performing made me so fucking nervous. What if I dropped a shrimp? Or didn't lick one long enough? These people were picky. They wanted the same insane amount of electronically generated whisper every time. If I fucked up, they'd send less money, but if I killed it, roughly the same number of them would be there every time. Whenever I thought I was growing my user base, the algorithm for the video sites I posted my eating videos on would knock me down to the same amount of engagement I had before. But I had to put the videos on those sites, as well as my own, which had extra videos for subscribers who wanted to shell out more cash, to make any money at all. I put up deep cuts and deleted scenes of eating. Eating blooper reels for the people whose thing was watching me drop shrimp on the floor. I ate to please.

I'd shelled out for a camera, an extremely sensitive microphone, the right lighting. Cleaning products to make my floor pristine again after shooting videos where I dropped food on purpose, and the videos where I did hero shit like eat cooked rhubarb off my arm in such a way that some of it would naturally and attractively float to the ground. I wore leggings to show off my legs when I filmed myself walking between the kitchen and the table, and white V-neck shirts to emphasize that my flawless eating techniques couldn't possibly stain a single one of them. I drew on cat-eyes with liquid eyeliner that made me look knowing and throwback sixties, like I might leave the dining table to sing a flawless melody with Mavis Staples.

I'd auditioned so many looks, but the audience had gravitated to the friendly, laid-back, approachable-girl-next-door-who-still-went-to-the-gym vibe. Truly, fuck the eating on cue, but at least it gave me an excuse to get out of sports bras and high-waisted athletic shorts and back into a real clothing lifestyle, even if my eating look was a little basic. The fifteen minutes that I spent before each taping putting on my outfit were the only minutes of each day where I felt alive. The rest of it was usually lost in the haze of preparing and recovering from eating. After downing pounds of food, my mind turned into a flat black sheet. I hugged my knees to my chest and leaned into the nothing behind my eyelids until my phone buzzed.

"You're coming, right?" Lanae texted me.

"To what?" I texted back.

"My show tonight? Don't tell me you forgot, girl."

"Sorry, I was eating."

"You still doing that?"

"I don't think anyone's ever going to pay me to do anything else."

"No, we're gonna get you back into the mall. I have a friend who works at the sporting goods store."

So it wasn't Lanae. If she'd told anyone about my stealing, it wouldn't look good for her to try to get me back into the building.

"Please, get me a job in the balls department," I texted.

"You wanna touch the balls?" she said.

"I want to stroke them."

"I'll tell her that. She'll hire you on the spot."

"Under my name tag, it'll say chief ball handler."

"So you don't want to do it."

"Whatever, girl. I'll do whatever. I have to make money, don't I? You know the shrimp only pays some of the bills."

The blankness disappeared and left me alone with my other ever-present companion, humiliation. Humiliation and I got up together every morning, brushed our teeth side by side in my bathroom mirror, and went off to the grocery store for inspiration. Humiliation and I ate our paid and unpaid meals together and sat down in front of the TV every night to search for shows about people whose lives seemed worse than ours. Reality TV stars who spent their time on some scenic beach, pulling out each other's hair in rage. Chefs who had the gray-in-the-face look of people who hadn't slept in weeks and seemed more into yelling at their workers than turning out good food. Game show contestants with fatal allergies to answering questions correctly. After we'd taken in our fill of other people's mistakes, humiliation and I were free to wash our faces, go to bed, and wonder why we couldn't find anything meaningful to do for enough money to stop worrying about rent and keep the debt police off our backs forever.

In bed, humiliation tucked its cold self around me, like a hug from a freezer, and reminded me that almost four years had passed since the last time I'd even tried to alter a dress on a film set. A length of time so long that in any wardrobe interview I could manage to swing together, humiliation would invariably slide her cold hand up my spine to derail the answers to any questions the interviewer might ask me. I was dying to work with real clothes again. Clothes that millions of people might see, and copy, and feel moved by. But to do that, I'd have to find a way to truthfully present myself as someone with a long, more or less unbroken record of acceptable employment. It was easier to spend my days with humiliation, eating whatever the internet asked of me and giving up on what I really wanted.

"So can I pick you up at five thirty?" Lanae texted me. "The show's at seven."

"You bet."

At six Lanae dropped me off where she knew I wanted to be, outside the bar she'd play in an hour, so I could do what I actually liked to do at her shows: people watch. I couldn't stand the punk music she and her band played. It sounded like someone had soundtracked their own electrocution. Outside, on the curb, I could re-dress everyone who walked by. After a day spent eating, mentally putting people into better-fitting pants awakened my muscle memory.

I wore an outfit that made me feel more like my old self. The one that outfitted people for movies. The punks wore black, and I wanted to fit in to escape the notice of the debt police. So I wore black too. But I did it my way. An oversized black T-shirt pulled down over my left shoulder. Skintight black vinyl leggings with silver vertical zippers that ran up to my mid-thigh. A long black braid made out of someone else's hair, and oversized black sunglasses that I didn't plan on taking off inside. Everyone else going to the show walked past me in their baggy and ripped clothes, and I silently congratulated myself for having a real look. Is there anything more tragic than people in the wrong clothes? Never.

When the flood of people streaming into the bar dropped down to a trickle, I went in to find a spot in the back. The noise from the opening act hit me like a freight train to the chest. Everyone smelled like beer and desperation. If I had to guess from the times I'd bothered to talk to people at Lanae's gigs, a third of the room was struggling musicians jealous that someone else got a gig, a third had an almost psychotic need to relax after working a shift at their terrible jobs, and a third had just wandered into the bar because they saw other people wandering into the bar. Enough people stood between me and the drinks that it didn't make any sense to push past them. I was trying not to pay for things that I didn't have to pay for. Now when I imagined ordering a beer, I'd picture the row of shrimp I'd have to eat to pay for that beer, alive and doing the electric slide between me and the bar.

The first band stopped, and someone put on in-between music. Even the musical filler sounded like a stroke with a chorus stuck in the middle. I felt a pinch on my arm and turned around, ready to get arrested. It had been six months since I'd worked a shift at Phoenix, and five months since the uncertain nature of my income had driven me into hearing the on-camera sounds of food at the grocery store. It was time for someone with turquoise epaulets to tap me on the shoulder and start going off about my student debt and the moon being in Venus. Instead, I spotted Audrey.

"Hey," she said, like we were friends instead of people who'd barely put up with each other at a job for three years.

"Hi," I said.

"You come to these things?"

"I'm here for Lanae."

"Me too."

Since when were they friends? Yes, Lanae had mostly defended Audrey, but she didn't hang out with everyone she defended. And every once in a while, Lanae joined me to make fun of Audrey's emotionless tone of voice and obnoxiously chipper amount of runner's energy. We'd mimicked folding clothes like she did, with a ramrod-straight back and an uncanny ability to make shirts and pants into uniform little squares that looked like they'd been whisked in fresh from the factory. We'd ripped on her laugh, which always made me feel like someone was sneaking up behind me with a very rhythmic knife. We'd huddled up in my apartment getting lit enough on tequila to admit she was probably better at the job than we were. Yeah, I hadn't worked at Phoenix in six months, but surely people needed more than 180 days stuck together to find common cause, especially when one of them was insufferable.

"I don't mind punk music. You can really feel the passion behind it," she said, like she was critiquing an eight-year-old's art project.

"Sure," I said.

Would she even be pretending to be nice to me if she'd gotten me fired? God, I didn't know.

A round of feedback lashed my ears. I turned around, where Lanae and her group were standing onstage, and reminded myself that feedback was not a song, no matter how many songs Lanae and her group were probably going to play that sounded just like it.

"Hello, everyone!" Lanae said.

She paused to absorb a round of applause, and adjusted the guitar that rested around her neck. I never liked Lanae's music, but she and her band always looked cool. All four of them wore long, shaggy black weaves, black stretch pants, and band T-shirts that were artfully ripped at the shoulder and in the middle of the torso. They all put on enough black and glittery gray eyeliner to look haunted, and Lanae one-upped the rest of her girls by drawing black slashes across her cheeks where blush would normally go. Their sound was an industrial tragedy, but their look sharpened up the Supremes. Made them edgy and vampiric.

"Let's show some love for our opening act, the Sore Throats!"

I clapped along with the room. Let's go, illness!

"If you haven't come out to hear us before, I'm Lanae, and my group is called the Donner Party."

Audrey and I screamed along with the screamers. I also enjoyed the shit out of the gaspers, the groaners, and the people who were familiar enough with California history to lean into their friends and say, "What the fuck." The best part of every one of Lanae's band's sets was the reaction they got after they told everyone they were a cannibalism tribute band. Lanae and the other three Black women in her group quickly launched into what, for me, was always the worst part of the night: the actual music. Tonight's set sounded like a cross between sweater static and an ear exam turned up to a volume that would kill squirrels.

Except that after the initial blast, I stopped hating the music. It was a relief to be away from my apartment and its aromatic reminders of my new day job and down here in the pit of a bar, with everyone else's sweat and elation. I couldn't make out any of the words. If you'd asked me to tap along to the rhythm, I might have imitated a seizure. Even though I had no idea what was going on, energy flew into my chest and through my arms until I had to put my hands up. Tonight the music felt obliterating, and I lived the kind of life that left me wanting to be obliterated. I looked over at Audrey, who felt it too. She dragged her head around in circles to the beat. We shook our hips, we tapped our feet, we looked up to the ceiling of the bar as if it was the sky on a quiet summer afternoon. Lanae and her group switched to another song, and just like that, I switched to a different, equally pleasant wavelength. I still couldn't understand anything she sang, but words felt irrelevant.

I'd missed the full-body high of listening to the right music. When we got out of here, I'd put on the stuff I preferred. Mostly seventies and eighties music and trap. Over-the-top music. Music that wouldn't stop letting me know how good it was. I liked a big hi-hat. A bass line that could control a summer. A keyboard that wouldn't stop until it reached world domination. If I was to live a small life, stuck in my apartment with a pantry full of our nation's crunchiest foods, the music I listened to could be bigger than that. I looked up at Lanae, shrieking into the mic with sweat flying off her face, and wondered when I had become so unambitious. Except I knew the answer to that question.

I lost my ambition a few years back, on the set of a movie called *Birdfeeder*, about birds who went feral when they ate birdseed that had turned radioactive thanks to a chemical spill. It was supposed to be an "energetic" remake of the Alfred Hitchcock movie *The Birds* that had profound things to say about nature, if nature was four trees at the end of a suburban cul-de-sac. But something about watching birds eat birdseed that they'd green-screened into looking like poisoned Grape-Nuts didn't say elegant.

The lead actress had tried for years to escape the specter of her dad, who'd spent forty years doing movies where he'd tortured masculinity to the point of death. He'd played a guilty soldier, an alienated suburban dad, an evangelical preacher afraid he'd stopped knowing how to guide his flock. He'd done worry, and sadness, and shame, all while drenching himself in the very convincing kind of sweat that had been reapplied every fifteen minutes with a spray bottle. It was good-looking sweat. I didn't really believe in actors beyond their ability to wear clothes I chose for them, but I'll admit her dad was hot. When I went back and watched the movies he'd done before I was born, sometimes I'd lose track of their plots and imagine myself licking that sweat.

If he was a fire burning his way through the spectrum of male anguish, his daughter was a Popsicle on a subzero day. She looked like him and everything, but the effect was as if someone had poured water over the match. While he wrapped up one of the most decorated acting careers of all time, his daughter battled vampires. Or aliens. Or dystopian animal-human hybrids trying to survive on a planet that was about to boil everyone alive. There's nothing wrong with genre work. But she hated it.

There are stretches on set where there's nothing to do but talk about people. The people you've worked with. The people you used to work with. The juicy rumors about the people you haven't worked with yet. So I'd heard all about her before I met her. I'd heard that she did shit like try to sneak Plato quotes into a killer dinosaur movie. Or pitch scenes where instead of everyone settling their differences via space laser, they just talked it out. Oh, we all knew what she was trying to do, from our positions in wardrobe, or behind the craft table, or in the prop room. And man, nobody cared. We were all there to do our jobs. She was the kind of actress where when she showed up on your set, the job was to help her slay that dragon in the middle of the desert full of quicksand before the Wi-Fi switched to the frequency that would kill everyone.

When I met her on the *Birdfeeder* set, she eyed me, and I understood. She didn't want to meet me for the same reason she didn't want to meet anyone else there. This wasn't a movie that would leave her crying grateful tears on an award stage, or even create a dedicated army of fans who demanded the movie be shown at midnight every Saturday in a theater with peeling walls and an aroma of rotting peppermint candy. It was just a job, like putting seat belts in a car would have been if seat-belt installers worked within sight of catering tables. And for her, that wasn't enough. She didn't want a job. She wanted what her father had. A springboard to world domination.

I took one look at her and knew we had a problem. No, not an attitude problem. You don't have to like your job to do it well. A fit problem. I had a rack of understated sixties wear in my trailer, all in the size four she said she was. Except the woman in front of me was at least a six. Some people took that kind of news well, and others did not. She looked like the latter. But maybe I was wrong! I so very badly needed to be wrong.

I welcomed her, took her back to the clothes, and began the process of trying to be gentle about it. Weight gain happens! I gained the freshman thirty-five in college because, as a broke person, free pizza was my lord and savior. During that period of worship, I adjusted the cut of my pants and embraced one of the major advantages of going up a cup and a half in size up top: darts. Darts are the missile silo of the dress. A mostly hidden show of strength and force contained in a couple of stitches of fabric. I enjoyed having breasts for the year of my life that weight stayed on, and I mourned them for a year after that when they left. Weight gain is not a tragedy. It's simply something that calls for adjusting to a new set of angles in your clothes. But the actress gave me the eye of death when I mentioned letting out the seams in the array of mid-century shift dresses she had to wear.

And so I didn't let them out, because she wouldn't let me. Whenever I brought it up, she would grumble me down. Whenever I picked up a seam ripper, she gave me a look that could start a fire. I even stayed late one night, hours after everyone else had gone home, to try to secretly do the alterations with nobody anywhere near me. I had just walked through the set to triple-check that no one was there. I had made it back to my trailer and picked up the dress, ready to prevent disaster. But she busted in.

"I left my water bottle here," she said.

"Did you," I said.

She looked at my hands.

"I know what you're doing," she said.

I didn't say anything. What the hell was I gonna say? My lap was full of dress. My right hand held a seam ripper. The table to my left held the matching swath of green fabric that would save the day. But she'd caught me in the bank with the bag of cash over my shoulder and the gun in my hand.

"And you don't need to do that," she said.

"Are you sure?" I asked in the most polite voice in my repertoire.

"I fucking hate you," she said.

She grabbed her water bottle from the desk near the trailer door and flounced out.

Girl, same, I said to her in my head.

I just sat there, with everything that I needed to wave off the storm in my lap, unable to do it. If I altered the dress, she'd notice. If she noticed, she might yell at someone more important than me. It was one of those situations where I was pretty sure making the right choice would get me fired, and making the wrong choice would also get me fired. I put the seam ripper back in my kit, put the dress back into its plastic zipper bag, and went home, hoping for the miracle of not getting yelled at the next day, and hating her for every single foot of the twenty-five-mile drive.

I'll never forget the dress that took me down. Lime green to match the radioactive birdseed, with fitted shoulders, but fairly loose through the body, hitting just below the knee. A cool-drink-on-a-summer-day dress. If she would have let me let it out, it would have lain the way it was supposed to instead of pulling over her top half in a way that gave her linebacker vibes. She would have given off the cool competence the movie demanded. She would have looked like a woman who could be as calm as possible in the face of deadly radioactive birds. But she linebackered her ass out there instead.

I had just grabbed a bagel from the craft table that was so dry it tasted like it had been born in desert sand when I heard it. A pop, and then a wail, like a little kid who'd lost their balloon. I gingerly crept over to the set and saw her half-naked, holding the fabric that was left up to her chest for modesty. But she'd busted out the whole back seam, so her ass was just hanging out there, getting some sun.

The rest of the crew stared at her with the particular passive face that has touches of amusement around the edges as they tried not to laugh. Oh, we all hated her. In addition to not letting me take out the dress, she complained about the food, about the shooting hours, about the script. Anything she thought she could get away with complaining about without getting fired. And the whole time I'd laughed at her behind her back, since no matter how much she made us miserable, she could never make anyone more miserable than she was.

But all of a sudden she spun around.

She was pointing at me.

Holy shit, no!

"This is Jada's fault," she said. "She refused to take this dress out."

Everybody worth their salt should have known she was being ridiculous. Why would I want her to look bad? I was a professional. I didn't have to like her to want her to look like the best damn radioactive-bird-fighting badass in existence. I never wanted this for her. The humiliation, the shame. The public nakedness.

But the director called me over. My ten-year-long career lasted another three minutes.

In the years since, I'd heard that pop everywhere. When other people ate. The sound of a rock jamming itself up against the outside of a hard-soled shoe. A distant gunshot. Just then, as Lanae started up another song, I heard that pop and turned around like the person behind me had lit a firework. Who the fuck chews gum at a concert?

The moment really died when I heard someone in front of

me shout over the music, "Can you believe the fucking debt police?" to a second person, who shuddered. On some level, I got it. Everyone in the room was the right age to have student debt. But could I not have a single night away from home without thinking about those Southwestern-looking motherfuckers? Suddenly I was drowning in sweat and loathing all noise, in a bar that smelled like beer that had been brewed in somebody's armpit. Here I was, a fired costume designer, doomed to eat three pounds of potato chips tomorrow that wouldn't earn me enough money for me to even attempt to make the minimum payment on my student loans.

After the show, Audrey and Lanae came over to my apartment, where I offered them self-dried mangoes and cheap tequila. If we'd made it home an hour before we did, I would still have been floating. When Lanae asked how it was, I would have been able to whip out some enthusiasm for Afro-punk for the first time in my life. But by the time we'd made it back to my place, I was at low tide. So I expressed some microwaved enthusiasm about Lanae's set, and the two of them sat down on the floor. I turned on my speaker and put on my favorite feeling-like-shit album, *Peter Gabriel 3*. Why the hell hadn't anyone else made an album with sour keyboards, bass lines that hit you in the head like a baseball bat, and lyrics about crime, losing it, killing people, and Steve Biko?

The music came on, and right as I began to bathe in its perfection, Audrey and Lanae both stared at me.

"What is this?" Audrey asked in a tone that let me feel satisfied, since I'd never wanted to drink with her anyway and had no idea why she'd just hopped into my car after the show like we were friends. Hopefully my musical taste had offended her badly enough that she'd want to leave.

"Peter Gabriel 3," I said.

"Intruder" detonated all over my living room, and its creaking-floor sound effects were making me miss stealing shit. I was more of a jewelry lifter, but I couldn't depend on people to leave their crown jewels within my reach anymore. Sometimes I dreamed about a more reliable way to know where rent was coming from so I could relax a little. Maybe even enough to start hitting the loans again. Not breaking into people's houses, like Peter Gabriel was doing in the song, but maybe something chiller and less likely to get me shot on the spot, like lifting people's credit card numbers from the payment stations at gas pumps. I'd seen people do it, and combed the news for evidence that anyone had caught them, but the cops of the world seemed to be going after other crimes, like failing to pay for college with one enormous check.

"Got it," she said.

"You don't know who Peter Gabriel is, do you?" I said.

We were all a good fifteen years too young to really appreciate the dude in his prime.

"Nope," she said.

"A sellout," Lanae said. "A man who drifted farther and farther away from punk."

"He was never punk," I said.

"There was something anti-system about his earlier stuff. He was a deconstructionist."

"But not loud enough for you. You want someone to come over to your place and personally punch out your eardrums."

"Is this song about stealing stuff?" Audrey said.

"Yeah," I said.

"Can't you see why she's into it?" Lanae said.

I could live without her reminding me why I'd lost my job. Peter Gabriel was singing about finding things in someone's cupboards and drawers. Let me dream of doing that, in 1980, when that album came out, and rents were low enough that maybe I could find something in someone's drawers to cover a month or two.

"Work isn't the same without you," Lanae said to me.

"Well, then it's weird that you turned me in," I said, testing her.

"I didn't," she said.

"Neither did I," Audrey said.

I looked at her, stunned.

"But you rip on me all the time," I said.

"Why would I sell you out to some people in corporate I don't care about?"

"You know," Lanae said, "right before he died—"

"No," I said. "Absolutely the fuck not."

"I saw him in the back room ten minutes before he hit the floor. He was eating his hard-boiled eggs and looking at security tape with you in it, making some motions in a fitting room," Lanae said.

My whole head screamed. Not Richard. Not the guy who'd made my life bearable for years after I lost it all. Not him. No. Never.

I got up and left the room and looked out the window next to my bed and cursed his dead ass. *Richard,* I silently said to him, *how could you do this to me? I hate green peppers. I'm sick of eating them for the crunch.*

Richard was up there in the sky in a double-breasted power suit, laughing at me for getting caught.

"Jada," Lanae yelled from the couch. "It's just a job that doesn't pay that well."

"How do you not get bored, or frustrated, or just angry that you're not making more money?" I said, walking back to them. "How do you not just quit?"

"It's easier to go in than try to find another job," Lanae said.

"You're the person who wanted more from working at a mall. Every day I just want to earn some money, get out of there, go on a run, and go to sleep. I don't have some burning desire in life or a long-term goal," Audrey said. "I just keep going. I don't mind the constant rhythm of days."

"You have no bigger ambition?" I said.

"What is there to aspire to? The planet's gonna melt. Food prices keep going up. I screwed up my other career, so I'm never going to be able to afford to move out of my mom's place. I don't know anyone who does anything fancier than what I do, and even if I did, am I supposed to want to be their assistant forever?"

"Girl," Lanae said, "how can you live without dreams? I can't. Even if it never happens, I have to believe that someday me and my band are going to be fancy as hell. We're going to be requesting spring water on our rider, and I'm going to have a house with a kidney-shaped pool and a set of servants that only wear yellow. Or at least someday I'm going to go home and go to sleep and dream about something other than the smell of that caramel corn they sell at the popcorn joint."

"I want to have a dream like yours instead of fantasizing about whether beef jerky or celery has a better-sounding snap when I bite into it," I said.

"You work in food now?" Audrey said.

"You could say that."

"She eats for money," Lanae said.

"What does that mean?" Audrey said.

"It means I fire up my laptop camera and lick food gently into an enhanced microphone for guys who, unlike normal people, are too hip to have a foot fetish," I said.

"Nope," Audrey said. "I simply do not believe you, because that's ridiculous."

"We're a growth industry."

"That's disgusting."

"Not all of us can have glamorous low-paid jobs at the mall."

"I'd rather fold clothes than deep-throat cucumbers."

"Jesus, you people," Lanae said. "I'm gonna pour you another shot. Shots solve everything."

Audrey and I grimly accepted our new shots. She took hers down. I felt like I had to match her. She poured herself another shot. I did too. When those two kicked in, the living room lifted itself ever so slightly off its moorings and began to rotate on an axis, but if I closed my eyes very briefly, I could stop it. Except the second time I closed my eyes, I saw Richard back there, dressed in yet another power suit, making fun of me for being a thief. I opened them.

"How is there anything worth envying about working for someone else?" Lanae said. "They never pay you what you're worth, and you have to go in there every day like you're trying to win the award for being the nicest person at a beauty pageant. Shit, girl, I wish I could make money by eating shrimp. You don't have a boss!"

"I wish I could make more money doing it," I said. "I'm afraid the debt police are going to get me."

"They got Christopher," Lanae said.

"Worse than they got him at the party?" I said.

"Yeah. I ran into him in Highland Park, and he told me that after the party, the cops marched him down to the bank at gunpoint and drained his bank accounts."

"That's fucking awful," I said.

"Did that pay his debt?" Audrey said.

"No," Lanae said. "But they said he made a substantial payment. He has Richard's debt too. They assigned it to Christopher after his death. The debt cops took their savings, and Christopher's bakery money too. It's all gone. He says he's selling the house and the bakery and moving back home to Atlanta. He's still crushed about Richard, and he's hoping to throw them off his trail by moving. On top of all that, he was limping when I saw him."

"They kicked his ass too?" I said.

"He wouldn't say," Lanae said. "He didn't want to talk about it."

"I still can't believe they humiliated him like that," I said. "In front of all his friends. At his party. It's like they erased his life."

Even if Richard had turned me in, nobody deserved the debt police. I pictured his fantastic house, bought up by one of those rich people who seemed to be flooding Highland Park, in search of colorful little houses they could paint gray. They'd strip down the interior, too. Get rid of the Miami bathroom and that otherworldly backyard fountain. Turn all that style and grace into an office with a yard.

"Since when do they take all your money at gunpoint?" Audrey said.

"Since they decided harassing people in person would be more fun than draining their bank accounts remotely," Lanae said. "You haven't been reading the news? Apparently not paying your loans back is criminal behavior, so they can treat you like shit, because nobody cares about criminals."

"There's a law about this that makes people who can't pay their loans criminals?" I said.

"Like they need a law. They're cops. All they want is to fuck with people," Audrey said. "I do not fuck with those people. I can't make my student debt payments, so I change lanes when I see them driving behind me in their turquoise cars."

"I know this is the wrong thing to pull out of that, and I'm sorry," I said. "But they drive turquoise cars?"

"Yeah. Black ones too, but every once in a while, you see a group of them in a turquoise car. Their Wikipedia page says it's a shout-out to the Southwest, where they're from," Audrey said.

"They have a wiki?" I said.

"Everyone important has a wiki," Audrey said. "Sure, theirs has that error message at the top that says 'this page needs to be changed to more neutral language because it reads too much like an advertisement,' but yeah, they have a wiki."

"Wouldn't a secret police force want to be operating below the 'have a wiki' level?"

"Oh, honey," Lanae said. "They're not secret. They very much want us to know about their New-Mexican-looking asses so we get afraid enough to make a payment we can't afford."

"Why did you think they were secret?" Audrey said.

"The idea of debt police is shameful enough that people might want to keep it quiet."

"You're living under the illusion that anyone gives a shit about indebted people."

Audrey was right. We lived in the kind of country where the minute you had any problem you couldn't shake, criminal or not, you were cast out of the light, free to receive whatever treatment the meanest people making the rules said you deserved. But on an emotional level, I couldn't imagine not caring about people with student debt. Not just myself. Whenever I heard that someone had the same kind of boulder on their neck for the crime of wanting to get a slightly better job, I always observed a moment of silence for our mutual position in the pit. But I wasn't going to pour my heart out to Audrey, a person who I'd hung out with exactly once, so I went back to my home turf.

"Anyway, turquoise cars look terrible," I said.

"They're like Mary Kay ladies, but cops," Lanae said.

"Without all the weird skin-care products that don't work," Audrey said.

"And they're just going to get an entire generation of people? We all have loans," I said.

"Multiple generations of people? It's so easy to lose your job, and not find another job, and have to go back to school, and get under their thumb again," Lanae said.

"I had just come to terms with the fact that I was never going to pay it all back," I said.

"That's not how it works," Audrey said.

We all hung out there, in our doom, getting to know it. The album had looped around to "Games Without Frontiers," and right when Peter Gabriel sang, "If looks could kill, they probably will" I saw the cops at Richard's house, giving us all the eye in their search for Christopher. Looks were killing out there. Or taking all our money. I'd spent the last three years hiding out from my own failure, but right then I felt the urge to punch a cop. I would never do it. I just wanted to enjoy the wanting to. Fuck the debt cops, and their crystals, and their astrology, and their turquoise cars, and their habit of taking people hostage.

"I hate this," Lanae said. "I have really tried not to believe in a system that will leave me indebted forever."

"Yeah, but what can you do?" Audrey said. "I know you're a down-with-the-system type, but when the system pins us under its boot, what are we supposed to do?"

"Ask your parents for money?" I said. "I can't, because I don't know who my dad is and I don't fuck with my mom, but couldn't you two?"

"Oh, my family doesn't have any money," Lanae said. "They're just trying to pay their own bills and maybe get to retire in their nineties."

"My mom doesn't know that I was assigned Dad's debt, and she thinks I still have a fancy government job," Audrey said. "I never told her I got canned, because she was so proud of me for getting what we both thought was a stable job. I can't tell her I screwed up."

"But you live here," I said. "Not in DC. She hasn't figured it out?"

"No, she thinks the feds have a national security office in Glendale, California."

"Well, somebody's gotta protect Porto's," I said.

"We can't let the terrorists steal our cheap Cuban pastries," Lanae said.

"I'll toast to that," Audrey said.

We held up our glasses.

"To Audrey's beloved workplace. The national security office of Glendale, California," I said.

We laughed.

We clinked glasses.

We drank.

Another half a song went by.

"There is one way we could pay our debts," I said.

"Really?" Lanae said.

"Yeah, but if you want to hear it, we should put our phones in my bedroom. You know those things are always listening."

"What are you, a conspiracy theorist?" Lanae said.

"Oh, no, she's right," Audrey said. "Phones aren't secure."

"Is this your government security side talking?" I said.

Audrey just nodded.

Lanae gave me one of her patented *I know this is a bad idea* looks, but she, Audrey, and I turned our phones off, stuffed them under a couple of blankets on my bed, and replanted ourselves on my living room floor.

"Sometimes I fantasize about wiping the databases," I said. "If they don't know any of us owe loan money, we won't have to pay."

"That's fucking ridiculous," Audrey said. "We couldn't possibly find their records. They probably keep all that behind lock, key, a bunch more locks, a shit-ton more keys, and a wall somewhere."

"Didn't you used to be a hard-core hacker?" I said. "Couldn't you just find the loan balances and wipe them?"

"Look," she said, "I probably could, but it isn't worth it. Even if I could crack all the security they probably have, they'd find me, and throw me in jail, and then I'd be even worse off."

"You want to get robbed at gunpoint instead?" I said.

"I am not a criminal."

"Are you up-to-date on your payments?"

"No, but . . ."

"I know you think I'm a thief, but to the fucking debt police, we're all criminals. We're outlaws, spinning our pistols in our holsters because we're not gonna pay. How much do you owe?"

"Seventy-five K. Some of that's my dad's debt. And for some stupid reason, I went back to school to do a master's in computer science instead of just trusting my hacking skills," she said.

"I owe a hundred K. I went to a private liberal arts school. It was supposed to be better than public schools, but it was mostly more expensive," Lanae said.

"Jesus, honey. I went to college and film school," I said.

"Out with it," Lanae said.

"This is an embarrassing-ass number."

"Let's go," Audrey said.

"You're gonna think I'm a freak."

"No, I won't. I mean, how much could you have possibly taken out?" Lanae said.

"Two hundred thousand."

"No," Lanae said.

"Wow," Audrey said.

"The financial aid lady said on the day I went in to sign the loans that I was investing in myself. I was buying a better future. I spent house money on a degree that left me here, in my beautiful house," I said, sweeping my hand across my living room so Lanae and Audrey could take in the glory of living in a bug-infested one-bedroom.

"By far the best part of buying a house made of student loans is all the threatening letters you get when you fall behind on payments," I said.

"They would have to be dangling me from a crane over a swimming pool full of ferrets before I open one of those again," Audrey said.

"Look," Lanae said. "You just can't think about the letters or the debt police. I don't think about the debt police, just like I don't think about the regular kind. Who the hell can think about either one of them mowing you down and stay sane?"

"I can," I said. "I want them to mow me down. I want my arms to go flying off into whatever grass there is around here. I want to be destroyed so I don't have to owe anyone anymore. I'm sick of spending my life thinking about how I'm going to pay rent and my debt, when I can only do one or the other."

"So you want them to kill you in the only place we have grass: a golf course?" Audrey said.

"Someday they're gonna say we're low on water, and the golf-course people will demand we save it for the golf courses," Lanae said.

"As long as that doesn't happen before I get my amazing golf-course death," I said.

We drank some more. Our laughs got drunker too. They had off-key notes in them, honks, the occasional squeal. They sounded like we had laughed all the way through a slow-motion dive into a pool. The two of them didn't agree to wipe the databases with me. But after they'd both passed out, and I was in bed, looking at the city lights beyond my window, I found myself thinking that if I was going to live a shitty, debt-laden life, maybe having friends would make it easier.

Six

The next day, I realized hangovers are better spent at home than pushing a grocery cart through the store, trying to decide what to eat for cash. My head was split enough that every few minutes I'd run over my foot with the cart and be so thrown off by the pain that I'd forget what food was. Then I'd remember that I was shopping for my income and aim my cart down yet another uninspiring aisle.

Food didn't have to taste good. It needed to sound good. I'd walk through the store, eye its shelves and counters, and listen to what was there. If I stared at food for a while, I could remember all the sounds of its consumption. The potato chip aisle was always full. Lush, even. I'd already done potato chips three times this month, though, because they gave off satisfying pops and cracks. They were truly the fireworks of food. I lingered in the nut aisle for similar reasons. A fat almond had its own pop. A deeper one, like each bite of an almond could dig part of a tunnel to the next state over.

I left the nut aisle for the vegetables. Tomatoes were too soft unless I grabbed the unripe ones, which sounded like a snake slithering across a floor if I bit into them slowly enough.

I'd done cucumbers before, so I was standing in front of their tougher cousin, zucchini, wondering if it made sense to set aside my lifelong hatred of their taste because of the snap I could get off a raw one, when I saw a debt cop in the distance. He was coming toward me from the nut aisle I'd just left, dressed in the usual black but for the left arm of his uniform, which was entirely turquoise. Why was his outfit more turquoise than the last debt cops I'd seen?

I did the only thing it made sense to do in the moment, other than mentally judge whoever had sent the debt-police uniforms back to the wasteland of terrible eighties fashion: kind of slither along the vegetable aisle away from him toward the milks, so he could get whoever he was after. Milk wasn't worth contemplating. Chugging noises never brought in the cash like anything that crunched or popped did. I worked my way slowly past its pale, useless self, hanging a left at the deli meats and sliding deftly into the cracker aisle.

I heard running noises, looked down the aisle, and saw two Black girls and a Black guy fleeing the store, their shirts ballooning on top of their backs as they took flight. Fuck. They had to be running for a reason, and at my core, I knew what that reason was. But I couldn't leave. *Yeah, people, I get it,* I silently said to their retreating backs, but how many of us could the debt cops possibly be after at the same time? And I had to make rent.

So I kept looking at food. Hello to my friends, the crackers, which loved to burst into pieces when bit in a way I could amplify until each bite sounded like a mini earthquake. And their friends, the cookies that came in boxes. The chocolate chip cookies that had a crunch like thunder and the gingersnaps that lived up to their name. Except I looked behind me and the fucking cop was still in sight, oozing toward me like a worm.

I very calmly passed the crackers and veered into the cereal aisle, which was halfway to the door. A hand gripped my forearm. When I dared to turn around, I froze. A white astrology cop with suspiciously good hair was eyeing me with a smirk. Those fuckers. They must have made debt police attractive so I would freeze for the tiniest fraction of a second, thinking sinful thoughts, instead of doing the right thing and sprinting out of the grocery store on sight like everyone else.

"Jada Williams?" he said.

"Oh, no," I said. "That's not me."

"Then who's this?" he said, holding out his phone, which had a picture of me on my last day working at Phoenix, with my arms full of the dresses I'd handed my last customer.

In that moment I fucked up. I ground my jaw. I had escaped so many accusations at the mall by remaining as calm as a sweet summer breeze. But there, in the grocery store, I knew I looked guilty. His eyes lit up when he saw me concede.

"I'm going to need you to come with me, ma'am," he said.

He led me away from my grocery cart to the no-man's-land outside the grocery store, far from all the loud foods that might keep me in rent money.

"You've stopped paying your student loans," he said.

I said nothing.

"You're five months behind on them," he said.

Nice try, buddy, I thought very loudly to myself without opening my mouth. *Like I'm gonna tell you shit.*

"You know that isn't okay," he said. "You owe a debt, and you are contractually required to pay it back."

So fucking what. I had two choices: I could continue having a home, or I could make student loan payments. I passed homeless people everywhere I went, living in their tents covered with blue tarps that were trying and failing to keep out winter rain. They ate out of cans. When they tried to cook, half the time they'd burn down their whole encampment. But no matter what they did or whatever anyone in power said they'd do to help, every Wednesday, without fail, they were raided.

At the encampment right outside my apartment window, people who looked like traffic cops in their little yellow glow-in-the-dark vests would show up in packs of four or five to throw anything a homeless person owned into the back of a truck. Ominously, the homeless people whose stuff they took were never around to watch. I spent every day eating on camera to avoid the fate of moving from sidewalk to sidewalk trying to eat without burning my world down or losing everything I owned.

"And because you aren't paying your debt," the cop said, "the contract you signed allows your loan company to take extra-special measures to try to collect the debt if they determine that it's unlikely you will ever resume payments."

Like I give a shit, buddy. Nothing you could ever say to me would convince me to pay loans instead of rent. I would never willingly give up my apartment and move to the dark side of the LA moon. Most of the people I saw in the city walked around with a supreme amount of facial confidence that said they would never become homeless. You could see it in their sneers, and the visceral disgust with which they avoided homeless encampments that took up enough of the sidewalk that they'd have to walk around them. I wasn't enough of a fool to pretend that anything I could control separated me from a life on the street. And now this motherfucking cop was trying to close the gap on me. Fuck him. He said some more stuff, but what was there to listen to? I knew what he stood for. Since I hadn't been listening, I was surprised to find myself on my back, on the sidewalk outside the store, with a stinging cheek. Had he punched me?

My arm hurt. My other arm hurt. A couple of his cop buddies showed up. The three of them went to town on me with their turquoise uniformed arms. I wasn't one to back down from a fight, but I hurt too much to do anything by the time I realized I was in one. Besides, I'm a Black girl, and fighting the cops doesn't tend to work out for us. Even if they're stupid-ass cops who absolutely will not stop talking about debt or wellness or astrology while they kick you into next week.

"These Leo moon incidents are always the worst," one of them said while I daydreamed about leaving my body.

Incidents? I hadn't resisted. I hadn't done anything.

Kick. Ow. Kick. Ow. Kick. Ow.

"They never take responsibility for what they've done," another one said.

"We all have to pay our debts," another one said. "Once I paid off eighteen dollars of dinner I'd charged to my Mastercard. I celebrated by taking a weekend trip to Sedona."

Fuck him and his eighteen dollars he'd paid off. Eighteen dollars? Did I miss, like, five zeroes? And fuck Sedona. I wardrobed a movie there once, and it was just baseball fans there for spring training and retirees hoping that having a stare-off with the stars in front of their $600-per-night hotels would fix their marriages.

"That sounds beautiful," another one said.

They kicked me in the thigh, the arms, the chest.

"Just being debt-free among the red rocks. Nothing like it. I had a big chunk of amethyst with me for the whole thirty days I carried that debt. Crystals work."

"They really do. I rubbed a geode I bought three times counterclockwise for a month, and it cured my mother's cancer."

"That sounds so much better than all those corporate medicines."

"Yeah, all those people selling pills at Target are corrupt."

"Who would put garbage like aspirin in their bodies?"

"If you let them, the pharmaceutical industry will kill you."

A lot of people think they know what adding insult to injury means. But I'm here to tell you that it's getting the shit kicked out of you while listening to the cops who are rearranging your body celebrate poisoning themselves with turpentine because they're too high-minded to treat their coughs with Robitussin.

They paused their beatdown for just long enough that I thought it was over. I looked in front of me, where people's feet grew bigger and bigger as they approached the grocery store's front door, but none of the feet cared to save me. When people got close enough that I could see their faces, they all just looked away. I didn't know you could get beaten up in a parking lot and have nobody try to stop it. They were really all walking by, gaping at me, and going about their merry way. Cowards, all of them. Then one of the cops kicked me again, and I retreated back into myself.

"What are you going to do after this?" one of the cops said to another cop.

"Oh, I thought I'd go get one of those new mushroom facials. Something about the fungus in them is supposed to clear up your skin."

"Huh. I still get acne sometimes."

"This is supposed to solve that."

My shoulder. Jesus. Ow. Why?

I rolled away from the pain. Or at least I tried to. From my new angle I looked up and saw that one of the cops was Black.

"C'mon," I said to him, desperately, between hits. "You really doing this to one of us?"

"I made the right choices," he said. "And you didn't."

Kick. Kick. Kick. Kick. Kick. I wasn't lying down in a parking lot anymore. I was someplace higher than that, where I could wait this out.

It all stopped. They backed off.

"This is a warning," one of them said.

This was a fucking warning? This was what they called warning people now? I couldn't move.

As a goodbye, one of them spit on my cheek. Humiliation, my comrade in arms, swaggered up from whatever dark parking-lot hellhole it had been festering in to lie down with me on the sidewalk. Grocery store customers stepped discreetly around the two of us, like we were a milk spill in aisle eight. A second wad of spit landed on my cheek. I searched frantically for the cops, sure they'd come back. I looked over at humiliation, thinking she'd taken her role too far. But the spitter was a random white guy with a grocery bag in each hand.

"Welfare queen," he said.

The fuck? Loans weren't welfare.

"Freeloader," he said.

He walked to his car.

I very badly wanted to put my physical pain aside to dig up all the hate I had in me for him. The asshole spitter who'd decided my loans, which I contractually had to pay back, were some kind of handout from the state.

"You should pay your debts," a woman yelled from somewhere.

"Those handsome men were trying to fix you," another woman said.

Fix me?

"That's right!" some dude yelled. "Pay the loans back."

Who the fuck were these people? I hated every single one of them.

But as I sat there bleeding, the person I hated most was myself. That asshole Black cop was right. I'd made the wrong choices. It was my fault that I'd ended up here. If I hadn't taken out those loans, I could be living a perfect, debt-free life. With my mother. Who wouldn't want to live with their mother and her failed dreams of being an actress? She'd thought she was living vicariously through me until the exploding dress, but then the minute I lost my job and career, she suddenly didn't have any time to call.

In the other life, the one where I hadn't taken out any loans, I could be getting old with her, both of us grumbling over our gray hairs while I failed her in a different, less indebted way.

Someone stumbled into my foot. I had to get up soon. I looked around. Apparently, I was blocking part of the store entrance. People who hadn't just been destroyed by the cops flowed around me, showing off their healthy bodies that weren't bleeding at all. I just needed a couple more minutes of rest, and then I could get up, and see how bad I hurt, and march right back into the grocery store to buy loud, crunchy food.

Someone brushed my head on their way by without bothering to help me get up. I waited until I could sit up, stood on shaky legs, and limped to my car, where I lay down in the backseat, below all the unhelpful eyes of everyone grocery shopping. How had it gotten dark? I swore I'd showed up at the grocery store at noon. What time was it? I reached for my phone. But a wave rose up in my stomach, so I cracked the car door open to throw up a mouthful of food and blood and shut myself in again. If this was a warning, what the hell came next?

Seven

Despite the urge to lie in bed until all my parts worked normally again, I had to try to keep making money in the wake of the attack, since landlords don't accept proof of injury as rent. I slept for most of the week afterward, but for a couple hours a day toward the end of that week, I spackled on foundation until I looked like a haunted doll. Unfortunately, the people looking at me eat on video picked up on my new haunted-doll vibes and kept asking me what was wrong in the comments. I crossed my fingers that at least a few of the dudes were very turned on by injured women, but the whole pack of them were less forthcoming with their cash, even though I'd eaten the zucchini I'd limped back into the grocery store to buy after sleeping it off in the parking lot overnight like a champ.

I licked that zucchini like nobody's business! I enhanced the sound of each bite until I made zucchini sound hot! Me eating zucchini was smooth like a Sade album! Those zucchini sounds were going to make sweet, sweet love to somebody under a palm tree! But the thing about making money online is that the fans never want you to change your appearance. Not even a little bit. No eyebrow plucking, no new lipstick, no aging. Nothing. They were paying for an image unchanged by the forces of gravity or time. And I'd violated that rule by getting my face busted up. I could cover up my body bruises with clothes, but the cops had left me with a black eye and a right cheek bruise too. It's in bad taste to resent the people who give you money, but fuck every single one of those guys who were making me wait out the healing time before I could go back to getting paid.

I needed money, so it was time to do shit I really didn't want to do. I visited the dark web and ordered some shit I didn't want to order. When it arrived, I grabbed that shit, put it in a tote bag, and limped into my car. I threw the tote bag into the shotgun seat and tried not to look at it. If I didn't look at the bag, none of this was real. I was in no way hitting bottom. I just needed a way to make money that didn't depend on my face. I drove down Fountain, then Santa Monica. I wore a black baseball cap, black sunglasses, and a black turtleneck. Normal people were on the street doing normal stuff like buying street fruit and waiting for the bus. I was a freak, caged behind car glass, feeling as miserable as a person who'd fucked up my life enough that I had to do what was next should feel. The plastic in the tote bag thumped when we went over curves and when the car in front of us stopped on a dime like a scared deer.

Twenty minutes later, me and the fucking plastic arrived at our destination: the first of three gas stations without security cameras. The old guy behind the counter in the snack shop, like his two counterparts I would hit up next, had chosen not to have a single security camera to stare at. I'd checked. Who the hell operated a gas station without spending most of their day staring at a four-camera split? LA was security camera paradise. Every building had a camera tacked to every corner you could see. There were flat black security cameras that looked like someone had cut all the sunglasses in *The Matrix* in half. There were black mini globes tracking an entire world of people's movements.

I picked the pump farthest away from him. I got out with the tote bag over my shoulder and filled up my car. Right at the end, when the machine asked me if I wanted a receipt, I pressed no and snapped my brand-new black plastic skimmer over the card slot. It slid into place with a click.

I hit the other two gas stations and took a different set of streets home, just in case. My hand shook every time I tried switching songs on my phone. I'd loaded this one up with trap to feel better. The trap guys were cooking up drugs and bragging about it. They had a pride I wanted to develop someday. A real fuck-the-system-that-won't-let-me-make-money-the-normal-way thing. Or a look at me, I'm-the-baddest-motherfucker-alive-for-living-outside-of-all-this-basic-shit thing. I was just scared of not paying rent, but maybe if I listened to enough Gucci Mane I'd feel a braver emotion. Specifically, the pride I would need to do the second half of the work. Sell the credit card info online so I could convert it into rent money.

Everyone outside the car moved a little faster on my return, to match my vibe. They ran to their parked cars. They hustled down the sidewalk. Even the hand gestures they made when they talked looked bigger. More animated. I liked adrenaline. If adrenaline went hard enough, it could paper over shame. And man, was I ashamed. This was shitty crime. There's an elegance to lifting jewelry. A sleight of hand. A romance. It takes skill, patience, and steady balance to pluck a watch from a dark corner covered in clothes, and the reward is a glamorous sliver of modern existence. But this credit-card-number-lifting shit was everyday, garden-variety trashiness. I was down there with loser teens, Ponzi schemers, and Shaun King. For a few weeks, anyway. Until my face healed.

Yeah, I could have gone after a real job with hours and a schedule, but even if someone had said yes right away, it always took them a couple of weeks to officially stick you on the schedule and a couple more weeks until you got paid, assuming nothing went wrong. In the meantime, the first of the month would pass me by, and the landlord notes would start appearing on my door. I also had no shot in hell of getting hired until the black eye disappeared. If internet men, who liked literally everybody with breasts, couldn't find black eyes sexy, I had no hope for retail hiring managers with their square-toed pumps and grim little smiles. I drove. Strip mall, homeless encampment, strip mall, taco truck, strip mall, homeless encampment, strip mall, Korean barbecue, strip mall, home.

I left the car and limped up to my kitchen for breakfast. More dried mangoes, some yogurt, since I'd read somewhere that protein speeds up healing. Could I just dunk myself in a vat of yogurt forever? Could I suffocate myself in yogurt, never coming up for air?

My phone buzzed. I texted Lanae back to say she could come over, and was shocked as hell when she showed up looking about as busted as I did.

"You got a warning too," she said, limping over to my other kitchen table chair.

"Yeah," I said.

"They sent me home from Phoenix. Maria says I can't look like this at work. She says I look like a carny who got in a bar fight."

I looked at her face more closely. She, too, thought she could solve her problems with foundation. The foundation people swore you could just spin yourself a new face with some paste, a brush, and a dream. They'd clearly never had a black eye. Foundation was always such a borderline decision for a Black girl anyway. If we fucked up the color, we'd look like roof tiles that were staring at you.

"Oh, girl," I said, and held out my arms. "Welcome to the circus."

We hugged in the awkward way two women hug when they're trying not to fuck up their makeup. All tucked-back heads like surprised baby birds.

"You doing okay, money-wise?" I asked her.

"Kind of. I fell behind on my loans when we went on tour last winter. I have a couple months' rent saved, but I'm hoping to get allowed back into work. Even though commissions are down. I mean, who do you know who goes shopping for clothes in person anyway?"

"I don't really talk to anybody these days, and I can't afford to buy clothes, so I think you might need another trend-hunter friend."

"You not being able to afford to shop for clothes is like the rest of us getting stabbed."

"I'm just bleeding out on the floor here, trying to scrape together enough to at least hit the consignment shops."

"Me too. Just waiting to walk well enough to do shows."

"Don't the punks love heavy makeup?"

"I think you're thinking of KISS. It's so hot at the shows that all this would melt, and then all the hard-asses who come to see us would be scuttling up to the stage like crabs, wondering what's going on when my face falls off."

"If you can put on enough foundation that it all falls off in one big chunk, you're deconstructing music."

We laughed. Her phone buzzed.

"Can Audrey come over?" she said.

"Of course," I said.

Half an hour later, Audrey entered my living room, with a funky walk and a bruised cheek that looked like she'd dipped the left side of her face in a mud puddle.

"The debt cops got me," she said, limping over to a spot on the floor. "It's my fault for falling behind on the loans because I went to a friend's bachelorette party."

"Have you thought about never taking any more trips and also cutting your own hair?" I asked.

"Giving up avocado toast?" Lanae added.

"Getting another roommate?" I said.

"Making your own coffee?" Lanae said.

"So you've been reading the section of the debt police wiki that's full of tips," Audrey said.

"Yeah," I said, "when I'm not busy getting my ass kicked by them in a grocery store parking lot."

"At least they had the decency to beat me up in my own apartment," Audrey said.

"At least you didn't have to go far to rest afterward," Lanae said. "They got me backstage at a show. My bandmates left me alone, because they thought it was a hard-core fan, but then they just kept beating me up after everybody left. It took me two days to feel okay enough to go get my car, but by then I'd already racked up three parking tickets."

"Nobody lifted a finger for you," I said. "Me neither."

"Not only did my neighbors not give a shit," Audrey said, "but one of them tried to hit on the cops."

"Who the fuck hits on cops?" I said.

"People who like being beaten," Audrey said.

"You guys need to read the news," Lanae said. "No one will help us because everyone they attack is always described as 'acting alone,' like the next step after not paying your student loans is killing JFK."

"So it's our fault that we're getting beat up."

"Yeah," Lanae said. "We didn't pay our loans, so we don't have the right to an unmarked face."

"We just get to hide," Audrey said.

"It feels like we're putting up with this," I said.

"Well, what are we supposed to do? Leave the country? I don't have that kind of money," Audrey said. "Or that kind of drive, really. I used to be important, and now I just want to go to work, go home, go to sleep, and have fun on weekends."

"Look," Lanae said, "I can still play shows after this heals, which is all I care about."

"If we really wanted to, maybe we could do something about our debts," I said.

"Oh, honey," Lanae said, "not all of us are jewelry lifters."

"That's not what I meant."

"I didn't know about the jewelry," Audrey said. "I thought you only stole credit cards."

"Jesus, man," I said. "I'm not . . ."

Audrey and Lanae looked at me.

I'm not what? I'm not a thief? I wasn't collecting a series of stolen credit card numbers that second that I would see if I could sell right after they left? I couldn't imagine opening my mouth and saying, *Yeah, I'm a criminal, I steal shit*, but it wasn't like that wasn't true. The problem was that people who admitted to their friends that they were thieves were thieves. And thieves don't have friends, because you need to be able to trust friends, and who trusts a thief? I saw myself as someone who did the occasional unsavory thing so I didn't go completely broke. I wasn't a criminal mastermind. I didn't have operations. I just wanted to keep paying my bills.

"I've done some things in the past that I'm not proud of," I said, proud of myself for sticking to the truth. "But do you want this to happen to you again? Do you want to be beat up? Do you want to get your ass kicked by people who won't stop talking about how amethysts cured their back pain?"

"I actually never want to pee blood for four days ever again," Lanae said.

"My arm has turned some colors I didn't know were possible for Black people," Audrey said. "Sorry you got the crystals guys. Mine wouldn't shut up about Reiki."

"What the fuck is Reiki?" I asked.

"When someone puts their hands on your ankle and says they're redirecting your bad energy and then the next day you miraculously get a raise at work," Lanae said.

"At least, that's what one of them said before he kicked me in the kidneys," Audrey said.

"So what are you willing to do to make sure this is it?" I said.

"Can I think on that?" Audrey said.

"You don't want to go where this could be going," Lanae said. "Or do you?"

"I said I'm going to think about it," Audrey said.

"Did you work for the NSA?" I asked her.

"I don't want to talk about it. Also, I legally can't." She sighed. "But I know what you're getting at, and like I said, I'll think about it."

Eight

A couple weeks passed. My face returned to normal, even if my legs hadn't. I sat down in front of my camera and mic with both a full bowl of peanut brittle and an empty bowl in front of me. Back to work. This was a pre-tape, as opposed to a live show, so I didn't have to worry about their reactions on the spot. Step one: transfer bowls. I stacked the peanut brittle in the second bowl, going slowly to pick up the max amount of brittle-crashing-into-other-brittle sound. After I'd recorded all those crackles, I moved on to the eating portion of that afternoon's entertainment. I put the first piece of brittle in my mouth and chewed slowly to get the max amount of sound from it.

Time to become pure animal, done with thought, working off instinct, giving my audience a little open-mouthed chew for people who liked variation in their chewing sounds. Up and down, crack after crack until I'd gone through the bowl. I became a tiger, ripping apart its peanut prey. I finished the bowl, blew the fans an amplified kiss, shut off the camera, and waited for the recording to upload itself onto my laptop. I was half an hour into the editing process when it hit me that I had no idea what the hell I was doing with my life.

I thought I was done with ambition, but being done with ambition had led me here. Trapped at my table, eating peanut brittle for an audience of sickos while I tried to ignore the pain in my leg. Even if I had to stay in debt for it, I craved what I had before. My old life, back on a set, where I became a happy ball of light because I got to tell people what to wear. I'd fought for that life one job at a time, from World War II flicks to deep-space dramas to laid-back summer comedies that needed bright stripes to match their snappy moods.

Now I cowered in my apartment, afraid to go out and get my life back, and drowning in fear of food that crunched. As someone who was well aware that work is precarious and can fall out of love with you at any time, I didn't want to be someone who lived for what I did. But when I thought about eating on camera for the rest of my life, I felt my entire body scream. And when I closed my eyes, I thought of all the clothes that had given me life. The clothes were my source of income, my sense of self, my reason for living. The clothes were everything.

I went to my closet and put on clothes that would make me feel less useless. A yellow, full-skirted silk dress from the time in film school when I'd started sewing all my own clothes. It started out as a cost thing and ended up a desire thing. I just didn't want to look like anyone else. A pair of yellow kitten heels that nobody wanted from the time I worked on the film adaptation of a banana-themed legal musical called *Appeal.* A black shawl I could drape around my shoulders to cosplay being a person who lived in a colder climate. In the car I let myself think about whatever I wanted. My thoughts moved from the lingering roasted flavor of the peanut brittle to the question of what to eat for money next.

But as I drove west on the 10, a fresh flare of leg pain brought me back to the issue of how to avoid getting beaten up again. I briefly fantasized about marrying rich, except I knew the stink of not having a real job would rise off me the second I tried to meet anyone who bothered with sport coats, or whatever their California equivalent was. Polo shirts? And I loved my most unnecessary expense, living alone, more than almost anything else in the world. Especially because there were no other LA apartments in my price range with the correct amount of closet space. But if I could get rid of my debt, it would be easier to attempt to reclaim my old life, instead of shaking down everyone I knew while sporting a fucked-up face from whenever the debt cops hit me up next and trying to explain that no, my nonexistent husband didn't beat me.

The 10 ended and spit me out onto PCH. It was there, with the cliffs to my right and the ocean to my left, that I first pondered a real solution to my debts. My student loan company was called Bobbie Mae and Willie Sue, like the two of them would lend you money and then immediately report to the sock hop to square-dance. They weren't stupid enough to put their real address on the internet. After Audrey and Lanae had left my place, I couldn't let go of the idea of finding out if they had a physical location, so I fired up my VPN and went online. I'd figured that they wouldn't have an office, or if they did, it wouldn't be anywhere near us. Thanks to a combo of Reddit and the dark web, I'd found out that they were dumb enough to put their physical servers in one nondescript building in Downtown LA that we could drive to.

Lanae made Audrey sound like a mastermind who could wipe those servers and whatever they kept in the cloud too. If no one could find records that any of us owed money in loans, we wouldn't owe anything. But I didn't know how to wipe their system, or if we'd need to enter the building to do it, or if the servers had physical backups. Or if I could get the other two to do this with me. And the entire idea was crazy. They'd catch us. They'd have cameras mounted from the ceiling, or embedded in the walls. They'd be looking at our faces from twenty-seven high-definition angles the minute we got in there. And then what? They'd hit us with a hidden sprinkler system that would distract us until the cops showed up? Maybe the walls would mace us. You never know in LA, a paradise so laid-back that it was covered in "armed response" signs.

Another wave of pain went up my leg, and I remembered that the loan people had already gotten me. I couldn't imagine a lower bottom to hit than when I had to convince my busted arm to open my car's back door so I could hurl blood onto a grocery store parking lot. I crossed into Malibu, the land of hills, beach, and houses big enough to remind me that other people had solved their money problems by somehow getting truckloads of it dumped on them so they could feel insecure for only having seventeen bedrooms.

Humiliation tried crawling up, tired and gray, to suck me back in, but I couldn't do it anymore. I jumped when a turquoise car smoked past me on the left, with a debt cop in an entirely turquoise shirt going eighty miles an hour toward someone else's nightmare. When I thought of whatever those debt police might subject the person at their destination to, inside me rose a white heat. I needed to fuck them up.

Nine

I thought about it," Audrey texted me the next day.

"Come over. Let's talk," I texted her back.

She showed up a little after sunset, so at first, in the darkness of my apartment hallway, I thought I saw shadows on her face. But she walked in, and the shadows didn't clear up because they were actually fresh bruises that she couldn't quite cover up with makeup. I understood why she'd come to see me.

"Again?" I said.

"I'm not having a great week," she said.

I gestured to my living room, and she limped along behind me. We sat down on opposite ends of my couch. It was the first time I'd ever hung out with her without Lanae as a buffer. After we sat down, I kept looking over at her, weirded out by the fact that she'd bothered to show up to hang out with only me. We'd spent three years working together speaking to each other in the clipped sentences of people forced to be in the same room to earn money.

Though she'd thawed out, I felt the weighted blanket of our previous collective avoidance pulling me down by the shoulders. She'd turned off her phone before she left to come to my place, as I'd told her to, and I'd turned mine off the second she showed up and hidden it under my bed. It was just us, as far away from each other on my couch as two people could possibly be, with a bowl of leftover peanut brittle as an island in between. I grabbed a piece, passed her the bowl, and got briefly sucked into the odd feeling of eating food off-camera. I chewed more thoughtfully than I normally would. The smoke from the roasted peanuts and the caramel notes of the sugar took on a louder volume than the mechanics of what my jaw was doing or the sound that chewing produced.

"You're really a hacker?" I said.

"One of the best to ever do it."

"Do you still hack?"

"Nobody pays me for it anymore. I'm a little bit frowned upon within the community, but sometimes, on days when my running group doesn't meet, I go home after work and fire up my burner computer and see if I can slide my way into other people's websites, for fun. It isn't the kind of high-impact work I did when I hacked for a living, but it works the muscle so I can stay in shape."

"What do you mean by 'frowned upon'?"

"A lot of people run away from you when you get fired."

"I know what you mean," I said, picturing all the people who used to talk to me when they thought I might be able to get them on a film set, and how they'd all vanished into the clouds the second I couldn't. And all the people who I asked for jobs who said they had just hired someone or that they weren't looking for anyone in wardrobe right now, with that sudden downshift in their tone, like everyone around town had gone to a secret meeting where they stuck my name up on a whiteboard of people who were done.

"Could you wipe their system?" I said.

"Probably. I'd have to see what their setup looks like before I could promise you anything."

"Okay."

"I could design a virus that takes advantage of a vulnerability in their code and run it through their network, where it would erase everyone's loan balances."

"Not just ours?" I said.

"No. What's the point of only doing ours when we could solve a bigger problem? It's the same level of difficulty."

"Okay," I said.

I'd never thought about going beyond our loan records, but there was something tantalizing about the idea of cutting the whole problem off at the knees. After I'd driven home from my trip out to the PCH, with the memory of the debt police car that passed me still in mind, I'd poked around in the news for stories about other attacks. Every name I found hit me straight between the eyes. There were thousands of us limping to our cars and throwing up blood, all because we'd forgotten to be born rich. The way the news covered it made it seem like getting beaten up by the debt police was as normal as eating breakfast.

"Besides," Audrey said, "if we only wipe out three loan records, they'll know it was us."

"Right," I said.

"The keys would be finding and destroying whatever the physical server backup is and covering my online tracks so they don't know it was me. Also, I could leave them a message. Like make it so their website says something we want it to say, instead of what it says now, which is basically 'welcome to the place that ruined your life.'"

"So we'd have to get into the building?"

"Probably. There's no way they don't have a physical backup. There's also no way that we're the first people to have thought about doing this. They're going to have layer upon layer of security. They're going to be a cake."

She tucked up her legs and turned her whole body to face me on the couch, clearly interested.

"How would we get in?" I said.

"I can handle the online stuff. But getting in is your specialty. You get into places you aren't supposed to be and take things that aren't yours."

I was supposed to be in all those fitting rooms! I didn't yell at her. I worked there! I knew she was just summing up my skill set, yet every single time anyone brought up the jewelry thing, I felt like they'd stabbed me smack in the middle of the chest. But I shook it off, because she was starting to sound like a person who was in.

"You're in?" I said.

"I refuse to sit on my couch at home for the rest of my life, pickled in fear, waiting for another debt cop to walk through my mom's door."

She looked at me, amused.

"Let's do this," she said.

Outside my living room, the block was kicking up a normal amount of ten p.m. street noise. People talked loudly outside the fancy Mexican restaurant, where they waited in line. The teens caught up and ate their tacos on the hoods of their cars. The two lanes of traffic started and stopped thanks to the traffic light that ordered them around. This week's pre-sweep homeless encampment included a street preacher who ambled into the middle of oncoming traffic as if he were taking a casual stroll in a meadow with his Bible in hand. He pointed at the Bible and yelled, "There is only the Word!" while all the drivers gently suggested he return to the sidewalk by laying on their horns.

"You can't live there," I said.

"I'm not ditching my mom."

"You could live with me," I said generously, even as I crossed my fingers she'd say no.

"They could come up on me right here. Or in the street. Or at work. Or wherever. Nowhere is safe."

Of course. I was so stupid. They knew where we worked, where we lived, where we drove.

"We'll get rid of the debt police," she said, sweeping her hand across my living room like she meant all my furniture, "and then we'll live the rest of our lives. When they legalized weed, they got rid of all the weed-sniffing dogs. When there's no student debt, those dipshits and their turquoise uniforms will disappear too."

"If we pull this off, what will you do with the rest of your life?"

"I don't know. Maybe try to get back into hacking. I'd love to make more money and do something that makes me think. I want to solve problems that are bigger than 'what rack does this shirt go on?'"

"I always saw you sitting back there, folding clothes, and you seemed content enough, like you just liked order."

"Who likes working retail?"

"I loved it."

If I closed my eyes, I could see it all. My empire of caramel corn. I could stroll those disinfected hallways, huff the smell of that Swedish Fish, and snatch peplum-waisted shirts out of people's hands to save them from a dark future of looking like human shower curtains. It wasn't film work, but I liked my methadone.

"You're a clothes person. I could live every day in the same T-shirt and jeans if people didn't look at me weird," Audrey said.

"I don't understand you anti-clothes people. You've never wanted to have a look?"

"Nope."

"You've never wanted to become someone else because you put on a dress, or a veil, or a new pair of shoes?"

"I'm cool being me, in the exact same T-shirt and jeans, forever."

"I don't get it."

I didn't understand people like her, living their dry little lives, untouched by the fairy dust of fashion. People who didn't care to adopt a style weren't living. I couldn't imagine my life as a dead person. Someone who got up in the morning without anticipating the ultimate thrill of looking into her closet and wondering what to wear. No matter what life flung at me, I had a wardrobe to get myself through it.

"It's not your thing to get," she said.

The thing about Audrey was that she gave off a confidence I almost never felt anymore. I remember feeling on top of the world back when I put both myself and other people in the proper clothes, but now my dominant vibe was watchfulness. Rather than feel things other than dissatisfaction and the shame of letting the debt police get to me, I'd started watching everything. People, cars, city streets. As if I was looking for some clue that would solve the rest of my life. At least that way I might spot the approach of the debt police as they sidled up to my car for round number two.

I watched Audrey for a second, sitting prim and proper on my living room floor with her legs crossed, and allowed myself to think of the biggest question I had. Could I trust her? Anyone who'd offer to wipe servers for me couldn't be trusted. Nothing this illegal was a question of trust, really. The real question was, if I couldn't trust her, did I have a plan for when she fell through?

Ten

Some friendships are accidental. I'd moved from hating Audrey to meeting up with her to eat my spare potato chips and go to Lanae's shows, where the three of us came out damp from other people's sweat and smelling like we'd taken a bath in a blunt. I dragged them to a midnight showing of *The Royal Tenenbaums*, a movie most people loved for what everyone said. I liked all the stuff that came out of their mouths but was even more in love with all the oddball clothes the characters wore: those tennis headbands and fur coats and tracksuits that turned 2001 into an eerie re-creation of 1975. Not that I was alive in 1975, but I'd pored over enough old fashion magazines to feel like I could close my eyes and take myself there if I needed to.

On a warm day in mid-March, Audrey somehow convinced Lanae and me to come on a fun run with her, as if running could ever be fun. Audrey described the course as only three miles through a gorgeous, wooded section of Griffith Park. I guess I appreciate trees or whatever, but they look better when you don't have to run past them. Lanae and I huffed and puffed and groaned our way through the ordeal, while Audrey and her friends bounded ahead of us like golden retrievers that had just spotted a tennis ball. At the end, the four of them stayed chipper, leaning over to put their hands on their thighs with enough vigor that they could have bounced back up and done another couple of miles while Lanae and I glued ourselves to a stretch of grass.

Audrey hauled the two of us up so we could say goodbye to her other friends and head to a bar on Hillhurst. Lanae grabbed us an outdoor table and I, as a person who didn't go to bars out of the terror of how much they cost, went through the mental math of trying to figure out the cheapest possible drink. Except after a couple minutes of that, I said fuck it. I didn't want to get sucked onto the treadmill of thinking that one cheaper drink would make a dent in my debt mountain, because it wouldn't. So I went big. We'd just run, and the world's most perfect after-run drink was something called the California Republic. An entire state's worth of booze. Mezcal, vodka, triple sec, oranges, lemons, sugar, and a maraschino cherry on top. Perfect to forget myself in while noting its layers before remembering the existence of the much richer people around our table in their button-down white shirts and fancy jeans.

They looked like the sort of people for whom the world was one big office, and if they stayed reasonably polite at all times, they could spend their entire lives advancing within it. It was always fun to invade Los Feliz with my scrubby-ass East Hollywood self, to not blend in with them. I looked beyond them to the people walking down the street and froze when I saw a Black woman with vaguely familiar face bruises, as if she'd just had a bad date with the astrology cops. I couldn't stop imagining how she'd gotten hers. Whether they'd jumped her in a parking lot, or at her job, or in a restaurant with her friends, or just at home chilling, with her door locked, not even thinking about the possibility that some extremely manicured cops might force their way in.

Lanae and Audrey interrupted my staring by sitting down with their drinks. Lanae, a practical person, held a practical beer, and Audrey eyed the pink-and-purple paper umbrella that sat on top of a drink that shone yellowish-brown in the sun.

"What is that?" I said, pointing to her drink.

"It's called the Genghis Bomb."

"It'll kill you?" Lanae asked.

"And then colonize the table?" I asked.

"Hopefully," Audrey said.

"Don't worry. I can fight back with a fork," I said. "One of those plastic ones they have by the bar."

"So we're set," Audrey said.

"You be set," Lanae said. "I'm staying tired. How do you run all the time?"

"By putting on my shoes. I ran track in high school, and then I stopped running, but when I picked it up again, I bonded with my running girls. We're all ten-minute-mile people, which is key. The runs help me power through a lot of frustration."

Out of the corner of my eye I spotted another facially bruised Black woman trying to hide the damage with imperfect foundation. Jeezus. Other than the fact that pretty much everyone who wasn't a Black woman had some contempt for Black women, why did they beat us up?

"Frustration about what?" Lanae said.

"Being a thirty-nine-year-old woman who works in retail. I should be out there, protecting computer systems for a living."

Or hacking them, like you're going to do with me, I didn't say, since we'd never convince Lanae to join our plot to erase our student loans. Lanae had a life. She went to work at Phoenix, and she played her shows at night, and she'd never let anything I might dangle in front of her interrupt the perfect schedule she'd set up for herself. I could hear all her excuses in my head, from *they only beat me up once* to *I don't want to lose my job over this, since that'll only make it worse.*

On some level I understood why Lanae wouldn't join us. A heist isn't a trip to the beach. But I was thrilled to have Audrey on my side. We'd met up a couple times to work on our plan, and she'd let me know that she'd started looking for a good employee username/password combo to get into their system and start poking around in their code for vulnerabilities. We'd sat around in my living room drinking, and she'd sworn she hadn't felt this good since she was a fourteen-year-old girl hacking into websites for fun under the limitations of AOL dial-up. I just nodded and smiled like any of those words meant anything to me.

"Why'd they fire you?" I asked.

"Even if I felt like telling you," she said, "I can't."

"You stole files."

"You really do think about stealing all the time," she said.

As if we weren't thinking about stealing something together. Jesus. Like hacking wasn't stealing, if you thought about it. She was taking people's data! And their peace of mind!

"You said something to somebody," I said.

"Somebody important!" Lanae said. "Someone you didn't work with."

"Ha ha," Audrey said.

"We'll just call you Edward 'Audrey' Snowden," I said.

Audrey looked mad but didn't say anything.

"You really can't say?" Lanae said. "It's not like you work there anymore."

"They made me sign a book's worth of paperwork that says I can never talk about what I did. Stop asking."

People at the other tables started looking at us. I remembered a time, before I realized that I would never pay off my student loans, when I thought I could knock out my debt and move into a house a couple of blocks from where we were drinking. I'd costumed some movies that had won smaller awards, so my career could follow a perfect curve up to me dressing people for a movie that won Best Picture. Then I'd buy one of the adorable little houses up the hill. I'd have a small but tasteful backyard with a panoramic view of the city below us, and I'd mount a hammock between two of my backyard trees to better enjoy that view. I'd fill the house with tasteful pan-Africanist art and take to wearing caftans in the summer and handmade shawls in the winter, all underneath elegant head wraps. On days when I felt quiet inside, I'd play SZA. On loud days Tina Turner.

Lanae put her beer glass down on the table and snapped me back to reality, where I dreamed of a lesser perfection, without a house or caftans, but with a set of wiped servers and a new, debt-free life. Maybe an occasional gig back in TV or indie movies, if I could convince a few people that I'd never let a dress explode on set again. If they absolutely swore never to let me back in through the gates, I could become a personal stylist, the more upscale version of life at the mall.

Then I looked over Lanae's shoulder and spotted a third bruised Black woman, doing a little worse than the last two, trying to camouflage a limp as she walked down the street. Of course. Why wouldn't we be the main target of the debt police?

Ten years ago, when I was in the middle of a series of low-paying wardrobe jobs and I'd gotten the first inkling that my debts might be unpayable, I'd looked up who had student debt in this country. Black women ranked number one. First, we screwed up by not coming from money. Then we demanded the same education as everyone else. But when we finished our studies, they paid us the least, leaving us with higher balances to carry forward. Forever. So of course we'd be most of the victims. The debt cops could make an example of us. We were at the bottom of the social hierarchy, and the pay scale, and so whatever happened to our faces could be one more thing nobody really cared about.

I went back to my drink, because I couldn't worry about debt forever, even if spotting three other injured Black women on the same street freaked me out.

Two hours later we packed ourselves into Audrey's car and drove one neighborhood over to my place, where I led them up the stairs, looking forward to drinking a little more with them and maybe ordering a pizza. I put my key in the lock, turned it, and opened the door to find out that I no longer owned anything.

In the five hours since I'd left my place, a team had come through and stripped it down. All the way down. No couch, no dining table, no chairs. No bed, no food in my cabinets, no rack of drying mango on my deck. No computer, no mic, no recording equipment. No books, no rug, no plates, no dishes, no pots. They'd even yanked out the bookshelves, which weren't mine. My landlord was going to kill me, right here on my empty floor. They'd tried to rip out the kitchen cabinets, which they'd separated from the wall.

I ran to my bedroom with an insane amount of hope, but no, they'd taken all my clothes. All the skirts and tops I'd made in film school, when I spent the first year cosplaying as a fifties housewife. All the jumpsuits I'd made the second year, when I woke up every day and made myself into a reincarnation of Donna Summer. All the shirts and suits and dresses and hats and heels no one had wanted from film sets. All the thrift-store treasure from all those times I needed to redo my look on the cheap.

An entire life in clothing, gone, but for the shitty athleisure I'd worn to go running. This was it. My worst nightmare. Being down to a teal sports bra, electric-orange bike shorts, and a fuchsia short-sleeved moisture-wicking top. I'd inherited the outfit from the set of an exercise-based horror movie called *Ride or Die*, about a serial killer who stalked a Peloton class. It lived in the back of my closet for whatever emergency might require athleisure. I refused to believe that emergency was now.

I walked over to where Audrey and Lanae stood in shock, but I couldn't look them in the eye. I would have gladly endured another beating if it meant the debt police wouldn't take my clothes. I sat down against the wall that separated my tiny-ass kitchen/dining room from the living room and closed my eyes, noting that I didn't have to call them the kitchen or the living room anymore because both kitchens and dining rooms had things in them. I couldn't face an empty set of rooms.

"They left you a note," Audrey said.

"What?" I said.

Lanae stood by the front door, biting her fingernails, which she never did, because her fingernails were always painted black. Girl had a brand, and that brand didn't include eating nail polish. She looked like she'd read the note.

I took it from Audrey. It said, *Thank you for the hundred-dollar loan payment. Your balance will be credited shortly.*

"A hundred fucking dollars!" I yelled. "My life is worth a hundred fucking dollars?"

I screamed. My downstairs neighbors knocked on the ceiling, but I couldn't stop. I screamed for all my furniture, and my food, and the computer and mic, since I had no way of making money anymore. I screamed for my worthlessness, since now I wasn't even worth their hundred-dollar insult. I screamed for my clothes, which represented, depending on how I thought about it, almost two decades or my entire life, and style, and way of being. I screamed until my throat felt like I'd slashed it with glass. And then I screamed some more.

Eleven

I woke up on Lanae's couch. She'd left me a note. Apparently I'd screamed until I passed out, and my landlord had stopped by to add to the festive mood by evicting me, and Lanae and Audrey had hauled me here. Lanae had to go to work but said I could stay with her as long as I needed to, and should raid her fridge and do whatever I needed to do to feel better. She didn't want to know what I needed to do to feel better. I went to her kitchen and fantasized about really fixing myself. I would feel so much better if I threw all her plates on the floor and rubbed myself on the pieces until I bled. I would feel better if I poured all the shit in her bathroom on myself. Just covered myself with toothpaste and mouthwash and shampoo. Gave up on being a person and turned into a sticky block of unpaid debt.

What would make me feel better? Lanae lived across the street from a parking lot that fed into another parking lot, and it was lined with garbage cans that sat behind the restaurants. If I left her place and banged my fists on those garbage cans until I screamed again, maybe I would feel better. If I went into the restaurants in front of those garbage cans and hurled their food into the back alley, that might do it, especially if the food hit someone in the face who'd just gotten out of their car.

There was a thrift shop between two of the restaurants. What if I went in and re-wardrobed myself by force? What if I lifted enough stuff to recapture my hundred-dollar net worth? I could grab handfuls of clothes to pair with other handfuls of clothes and start over. I could come out of the thrift shop and wreck the neighborhood. I could drive my car into a pole. I could buy illegal fireworks and start blowing shit up. I could hurl food and explosives and myself at other neighborhoods. I could enter buildings and boutiques with glowing red eyes and burn everything inside them to a crisp with a glance.

I went to Lanae's kitchen, where I put on water for coffee and thought it was a shame that by doing whatever I needed to do to feel better she probably didn't mean smashing one of her mugs. It would feel so good to take a hammer to one of them and come up with one sharp ceramic shard to greet the cops who'd stripped my apartment, if they bothered to come here. I could carry my clay weapon and meet them wherever they were. Whoever they were. I could get my revenge. I could slash their motherfucking throats.

Whatever. They were the fucking debt police. I could see those guys in my apartment, in their immaculately coiffed hair and turquoise uniforms, taking everything I owned while one of them put on Jimmy Buffett and they all did mushrooms. I always imagined them going in for some self-care after they ruined someone's life. Maybe they went for pedicures to celebrate caving in the jaw of a twenty-five-year-old Black woman who'd gone to college and could only find a job in food service. Maybe they pondered water signs during a deep tissue massage after they punished a forty-year-old Black mother of three for the crime of going back to get her degree in history. If I ever found them, I'd kick their asses. I'd hit them in the balls. I'd grab them around their necks and twist. I'd . . . I'd . . . I'd . . . do nothing. I was five ten and might have weighed a hundred forty pounds if my pockets were filled with concrete. I would not suddenly get into the ass-kicking business. And if I tried, they'd beat me up again. I remembered sitting in the backseat of my car in the grocery store parking lot, where, even as a pessimist about how much other people cared about Black women, I was shocked when absolutely no one popped over to say something about how they agreed that it wasn't polite to try to kill people in a grocery store entrance.

The water boiled, and I wandered around Lanae's kitchen to figure out what I could make coffee in. I grabbed filters and one of those glass coffee makers that looks like it has a ribbon tied around its waist. I put the filter in, ground some coffee with her countertop grinder, dumped the grinds in the filter with hot water on top, and tried my damnedest to stop fantasizing about killing cops. But the second I switched my mind off cop killing, it insisted on thinking about how everyone else in the world who wasn't me owned furniture. Well, maybe they rented it instead of grabbing it off curbs on garbage day like I had, but the point was it was there, sitting in their bedroom or living room or kitchen, not being taken away.

Why had they bothered taking my furniture? There was no way it would be worth it to a loan company to snatch what they considered to be a few dollars' worth of shit. I owed so much more than that. I would never pay it off. They could steal everything of mine they got their hands on for decades without making any real dent in that balance.

I had gone to fucking film school! I had taken out all those loans I was never going to pay back! I was so fucking stupid! I should have just moved to LA after college and hunted around until I knew someone who could hook me up with a job! Except film school had convinced me they'd reduce the risk people took on to just move to LA without anything lined up and find jobs. The film school people had promised me that all I had to do was go to film school, where I would find professors who would hook me up with jobs, and I wouldn't have to take the risk of paying LA rent that I couldn't afford as a working-class person who wouldn't be sauntering into the city with family money.

At film school they could erase my working-class-ness. They could give me a glittering future. They could expose me to the glamorous, film-filled side of New York, even though the film industry is in LA. But it was uncouth to pretend anything wasn't possible in New York, and they weren't going to be the first. Yes, I'd have to take out loans to fulfill my end of the deal, but then film school would take care of me. Everybody there said so.

Then I'd discovered, much too late, that film school was about taking people's tuition money to study with people who hadn't worked in Hollywood for years and didn't know anyone who was hiring. So I'd ended up doing the thing I hadn't wanted to do. I'd moved to LA, paid rent I couldn't afford, and added credit card debt to my film school debt while I worked in boutiques and threw myself at every wardrobe or costume job in existence. I'd starved myself enough to eventually cover the credit card debt with retail money and film jobs while the mountain of student loan debt just stood there, mocking me.

Why did I belong to a generation of people who thought so many problems in life could be solved by going to more school? I'd fallen out with everyone I'd known from my college and film school days, but I remembered so many conversations about people who'd gone to plenty of school seriously considering the act of going to even more school to rapt audiences of people who cheered them on like attending more school was a baseball game we were about to win in the bottom of the ninth. At my high school graduation, the speaker had told us that high school was a gateway to college. At my college graduation, the speaker had said college was the glorious path to the middle class. And at my film school graduation, the speaker had said we were well on our way to taking over the world with our art. Where was my piece of the world? How had years on film sets amounted to me not having any physical stuff to call mine?

I poured the coffee and rifled around in Lanae's cabinets until I found some dried apple rings, which reminded me of my beloved porch-dried mangoes. The apple rings inspired me to cry into my coffee. Lanae didn't have any money either. She couldn't keep me here! We'd go absolutely dead broke together! I couldn't do that to her! She didn't need a roommate who didn't make any money and was going to have to come up with a whole new strategy to change that.

I finished breakfast and went to Lanae's bedroom. Since I'd lost all my clothes to the cops, I wanted to look at hers. When she'd said I could do whatever I needed to feel better, she meant borrow her clothes.

Her closet contained the all-black wall of clothing that punks were required to own by law, but it was a look, and looks were good. Lanae's black clothing had everything. Spikes, leather, vinyl, jersey. There were leggings and skinny jeans and sailor pants. Studded belts. Army boots and minimalist booties and Doc Martens and house slippers. A couple of nightgowns and a set of oversized T-shirts, because she wasn't one to give up on her style, even while asleep. An entire world done in black. Somehow, even though she was short and curvy and I was tall and skinny, we averaged out to the same size.

I knew she'd let me borrow whatever I wanted from her wardrobe, but instead of picking from the infinite blackness, I went for the one thing I figured she'd never wear. A gauzy polyester caftan with sixties neon Murakami-like pop-art chrysanthemums that someone must have thrown at her at a show and she must have forgotten to throw back. I hauled it out of the closet, slipped it on over my stupid fucking athleisure, and pulled it shut with its attached belt. There's something about getting properly dressed that lowers the blood pressure.

I topped it with one of Lanae's turban-like black silk head wraps and flipped on her TV to try to forget about my dearly departed clothes. After the game shows, the talk shows, and the soap operas, I found a very old reality TV show called *The 5th Wheel*, where two couples would go on a double date, and halfway through the date, a fifth person would bust into their cab or suddenly sit down at their restaurant table. At the end of the episode, everyone was asked who they wanted to go out with again. If anyone matched, the host of the show would congratulate them like they'd said they were getting married, and if no one did, they'd all leave with sour looks on their faces. A perfect show for a person like me, who had just lived through chaos. My fifth wheel was the people who had stolen everything I owned. Man, I needed money. I couldn't live here forever, and when I moved out, I'd need money to do it.

I took out the burner phone I'd bought after I installed the credit card skimmers, checked for a second round of credit card data, found it, went to one of the darker places on the internet to put it up for sale, and felt better. Fuck people who had credit cards. Soon, they'd feel at least some of the same pain that I did. As a person who now had nothing, I lived for picturing the moment when other people fell down in the shit with me.

Lanae walked in the door after thirteen hours of me watching finance bros bust in on dates between artists, and emo girls who crashed dates between hip-hop lovers, and absolutely no one matching with anyone. She dropped her keys in the bowl she kept on the floor by the front door and stood in the doorway of her living room without saying anything. I looked at her face. I couldn't move. They'd gotten her again. She walked over near where I sat and lay down on the floor, where I looked down and watched the purple spots on her face very slowly blossom into full flower. She turned off her phone and gestured at me to do the same. I turned off my phone.

"At the show, in front of everyone there," she said, answering the question I hadn't asked. "We were playing that new song of ours, 'Dysentery,' and halfway through the first verse they hauled me offstage."

"Fuck them," I said.

"I managed to crowd-surf my way back to the stage, but it's impossible to sing when your face feels like a glass bowl that might crack."

"I'm sorry."

"The crowd thought it was normal. People get beat up at punk shows! But not when they don't want it. Not when it's the debt police. How did nobody fucking stop them?"

I lay down on the floor with her, just like the day Richard died.

"Is there a way to end this?" she said.

"You know what I want to do."

"And I didn't think I wanted to do it with you."

I waited. If she was with me and Audrey, she'd need to come herself, without a single push from us.

She sighed. "I thought someone would stand up for us," Lanae said.

"You mean us Black women?"

"I've seen us everywhere. At the mall. At Echo Park Lake. Trying to hide it on the beach, like it makes sense to walk around with a full face of makeup on sand. I thought maybe the Democrats . . ."

"Would override the corrupt court system that keeps smacking their loan forgiveness bills down? They believe in following the rules, even when there are no rules," I said.

"Or the hard left, since it's cop violence . . ."

"They would prefer us to be white. They get all fired up about the cops, and I get it! I hate the cops too! They put those Black

Lives Matter signs up in their windows, and then, when they think nobody's looking, they take them down. We're in more of a Black lives don't matter era."

"I can't believe the universities don't care either," Lanae said.

"Audrey actually wrote her college about this, and they wrote her back, saying that it's not their place to get between borrowers and the terms of their loan agreements."

"Even though the debt police are beating us up."

"We made them money, and students are still making them money, so of course they're fine with it. They wash their hands of everything about us at graduation except for what we owe them."

"Wait, you and Audrey hang out?"

"She's not so bad."

"I told you!"

We sat in silence for a moment.

"I don't want to be a criminal," Lanae said.

"You already are. That's why cops are beating you up. You're not going to win an 'I'm not a criminal' debate. They are literally marking us whether we like it or not!"

"I really don't want to do it."

"Then don't do it! I'm not gonna make you do anything!"

"They're not going to get me a third time," she said.

I looked at her. She'd changed. Something had entered her eyes. A different kind of light. They'd really fucked her up.

We lay there on the floor of her living room, waiting. I had a job for Lanae in me and Audrey's plan. I needed her. My whole life lay in this round of silence. My right to protect my body and face, to go outside again without fear. I was too afraid to do anything other than let her talk. But silently I was cheering her on. *Come on, Lanae! You can do this! No one's gonna bail you out but me!*

She pulled herself off the floor so she could look me dead in the eye.

I couldn't breathe.

"I'm in."

Part Three

The Payback

Twelve

Audrey, after weeks of searching, found a set of usernames and passwords for the company's main loan officers on the dark web. One night after work, she came over to Lanae's without her phone to show off what that meant. Lanae and I turned off our phones and put them under a bowl in the kitchen. Audrey opened her laptop, went to the loan company's corporate website log-in, and put in a username and password.

"Their server thinks I'm logging in from Washington, D.C., where they have employees who work from home," she said. "All the employees here, where they keep their servers, actually physically work in that office you found Downtown, Jada. Do either of you want to see your accounts?"

"Sure," Lanae said.

Audrey clicked and moved around until we got to a screen that showed Lanae's balance and history of payments. Near the top I spotted a yellow exclamation point.

"What's that?" I said.

"The point where she fell behind on payments," Audrey said.

"Ugh," Lanae said. "Can we get out of this? I'm sorry I said I wanted to see it. I know how much I owe. I haven't stopped thinking about that number in years. I see that number whenever I close my eyes."

"Sure," Audrey said.

She left Lanae's page and wandered around the site until she found its underlying code, a list of numbers and letters and symbols that meant nothing to me. But she stared at the code with pride, like she'd given birth to it.

"Isn't this gorgeous?" she said.

"Kind of?" I said.

"If you're into this sort of thing," Lanae said.

"I am," Audrey said, "and let me tell you, this is some beautiful code. Almost airtight."

"What do you mean, 'almost'?" I said.

"They have vulnerabilities," Audrey said. "Holes in their code that someone could take advantage of. I imagine they have a great IT team, given how many people are interested in making sure we will never be rid of our student loans, but I'm surprised they haven't seen what I have. Do you want me to explain it to you?"

"In terms we can understand," Lanae said.

"There are a couple of tiny issues with their site that mean a bad actor, like me, could pop in and insert a little code to take advantage of them and wreck their system. But that's the obvious move. I'd probably want to do something a little more subtle, like draw up a bad email for someone to click on that would put a little code in their systems for me so I could hang out and figure out how to put together a bigger, more destructive act. I want to know more about the setup of the LA office, since we know they keep their servers there, to see if they have smart security, or smart printers, or any other electronics they link to their network that I could use to get into their systems and start working on a plan to insert a piece of bad code."

"So you can't rewrite the code you found?" I said.

"No," Audrey said. "I'm not in their system yet."

"You need us to get you in," I said. "I can do that."

"You can?"

"You bet. I'm an observer. I can watch people, figure out what their deal is, use the force for more than keeping track of jewelry people left behind. Lanae and I will camp out near the building and watch how employees go into and out of it. Do they use security badges? Are they punching a code in at the door? Are there guards outside, inside, or in both places? What time does everybody go in and out over the course of the day? This isn't hard stuff," I said.

"I need to come?" Lanae said.

"Yeah. I could tell you about the routine, but I think you'll remember it better if you see it."

"I can only go on my days off."

"No problem. Thank your lucky stars that you have an unemployed jewelry thief on the team."

"And a credit card number lifter," Audrey said.

"How do you know?" I said, mouth open.

"I hit two or three gas stations regularly, and I saw you at one of them, making too many hand motions at a pump. I'm not stupid. But you might want to get better at covering your tracks."

"When I'm done with this, you'll be calling me the queen of subtlety."

"I hope so," Audrey said.

We looked at each other for a heated moment.

"Chill out, guys," Lanae said. "We got this."

Fingers crossed.

Thirteen

"Where should we park?" Lanae said.

"I don't know," I said.

We were in my car without our phones. We had my car windows shut so no one could hear us. I'd been doing loops around the long Downtown block with the student loan company's offices for twenty minutes. We passed ten apartment buildings. Three Irish bars. Four parking garages. Both a casual and an upscale taqueria. Three guys on the street selling Lakers merch. Two sandwich boards outside bars that advertised both a happy hour and an hora feliz. Too many businesses and people to make me feel comfortable. Even though I knew the odds were against us, I'd been hoping for the one abandoned Downtown block in existence. A quiet place, where it would never occur to anyone that two women were casing a building.

"Maybe we shouldn't park?" I said. "Because we don't want to get out of the car and accidentally walk within view of one of their surveillance cameras, if they have one."

"This is LA," Lanae said. "They have one camera for each side of the building. At least. But if we park, we can see if they have a guard who sits out front or out back or whatever."

"We are so bad at this," I said.

"No, we're not! We're figuring it out!"

"We can do two more laps, tops, before they notice the car."

"They could have noticed any of our other laps!"

"Noticing a white Honda Civic is like declaring that there's a special piece of lettuce in your salad."

The only thing the debt police had left me was my car. For the life of me, I'll never understand why they didn't figure out the car parked outside my building and registered to my name was mine. Or if they had, why they didn't take it. Too busy arguing about which vaccines made your feet magnetic, I guess. White is the most common car color in the United States, and the Honda Civic is the most common car in California. I looked all this up once—after I bought it, since nobody buys a car with the intention of becoming a shady person. I hadn't meant to become this shady. But since I wanted revenge for getting beat up, having a common car felt like a pile of gold had dropped into my lap. Even so, LA was so full of security cameras, outside guards, and license plate scanners that I figured that me and my boring, unmemorable car would be recorded, even if we weren't remembered.

"I'm parking," I told her.

"Go for it."

I pulled into a spot four spaces behind the back of the building. Behind the building lay an alley, and at the end of the alley closest to our car I spotted a single black folding chair.

"So they've got a guard with a chair," Lanae said.

"Probably."

I made a brief sketch of the alley, the chair, and the building.

"You draw?" Lanae said.

"Before the costuming thing, I thought I was going to become a fashion designer. Designers sketch all their looks. I haven't sketched in a while, but I imagine we're going to want a diagram to work with so we can use it to memorize the inside and outside of the building before we have to attack it."

"There he is," I said to Lanae ten minutes later, having spotted our outdoor security guard. He was a skinny Latin guy wearing a standard-issue mall cop uniform, despite the absence of a mall. He looked too alert, like he might notice a paper clip tumbling down the alley in front of him. I silently fumed at not getting a guard who looked more like an idiot. He sat down on the black folding chair in the alley and entertained himself with his phone. I looked down at the watch Lanae had lent me. 1:32 p.m. I noted his presence below the sketch with the time. We'd have to do a morning stakeout sometime, but we'd both slept in, since it was Lanae's day off from work, and we'd stayed up late watching *Waiting to Exhale* out of that shared sense of being Black women in our late thirties who were basically preparing to pull Angela Bassett's move of setting a car on fire.

"Fascinating guy," Lanae said.

We both laughed.

"The back security camera is right across from him, on the bottom right-hand edge of the building," she said.

I looked. It was a standard LA security camera. The kind that was attached to the building like a big sticker, with a globular black lens. I drew it and also wrote its existence down on the pad of paper, alongside the guard. Then I absentmindedly checked for my phone, and remembered that we'd both left ours at home. Sometimes, when we went cruising around without our phones, those adorable little tracking devices that fit in a pocket, I felt like we were dirty private detectives in like, 1973.

"You think that's an employee?" she said.

I looked up to see a guy, white, blond, late twenties, wearing a short-sleeved dress shirt and khaki pants, come out of the building and walk down the alley away from us.

I looked at him through Lanae's binoculars, which she'd used on one bird-watching trip once, and also now. "He has a building badge attached to his pants."

"We're going to have to get one."

"And go in that door. The back is our private island, the front is practically the Venice boardwalk."

We were parked next to a row of apartment buildings. Most of the businesses and all the parking garages were on the front of the block. The front door of the office building we were checking out stood directly across from one of the Irish bars, and the problem with Irish bars is that there's always someone in them getting lit no matter what time of day.

A debt cop drove by in a turquoise shirt and hat. We ducked down in the car so he wouldn't spot us.

"Have you noticed that their uniforms are getting more and more turquoise?" I asked her.

"They're like caterpillars turning into butterflies, if they grew by taking more and more of your cash at gunpoint."

"They even have a Mary Kay setup. They steal enough money from people, they get their turquoise Cadillacs."

"You hungry yet?" Lanae said.

"I could eat."

I hauled a tote bag stuffed with food out of the backseat. She'd made us a car picnic lunch. Ham-and-cheese sandwiches. Some insane brand of potato chips called Zapp's Cajun Hellfire, since she was the kind of person who believed the more off-the-wall the chip name, the better the taste. I'd contributed some of the mangoes she let me dry off her back deck and two thermoses of water, since tequila didn't feel like the best drink for a stakeout where we had to keep paying attention.

It was a lovely spring day. Seventy degrees, so not too hot to eat with the windows up. There's something relaxing about chowing down in a car while you wait for a security guard to move. Ours didn't. Yeah, we can all look at our phones forever, but my bored self wanted him to find something to do. Come on, man. Check out a suspicious garbage can. Roll over to a dark corner of the alley to vet a threatening burger wrapper.

Then the chips hit me.

"What are these supposed to taste like?" I said.

"Whatever Cajun hellfire is? To me, all those flavors that sound Southern like that are basically just hot sauce."

"They should make more hot-sauce-flavored chips."

She clapped her hands together, like I was a sports team she approved of.

"I knew you'd like them," she said.

Just then, our employee came back. He, as we'd predicted,

used the thing that looked like a security key to swipe his way back into the building.

Right after that, our security guy moved. Lanae and I stopped eating, mid-bite, to watch him. He disappeared from sight down the part of the alley we couldn't see and came back. He did it again. A third time.

"What do you think he's doing?" Lanae said.

"Laps," I said.

"Oh," she said.

We went back to our chips.

Another hour passed.

Our security guard had been perched on his chair for most of it, as if getting up was a childish fad.

"Do you ever wonder what you'd be doing if you hadn't taken out the loans?" I asked Lanae.

"Yeah. Sometimes I imagine myself doing something crazy, like learning to sail ships. Or traveling the world."

"I used to fantasize about being a cook," I said.

"You? The person who lives on dried mangoes and tequila?"

"If I wasn't poor, I would eat everything. Teach myself how to cook all of it too."

"I just can't see you as a cook."

"Yes, you can. You can see me, all crisp in chef's whites, turning out slivers of translucent fish that look like sea glass on the beach next to tasteful little bundles of vegetables and herbs. It's all detail work," I said. "I love details."

"True," she said. "Sometimes I fantasize about gardening."

"You're never home!" I said.

"Yeah, but if I didn't have the debt, I'd have more money. Then I could be home, with my little nursery of tropical plants that I'd have time to take care of between gigs."

"Wait, he got up," I said.

We were silent for a second, watching the guard take a few steps down the alley.

"That's the worst thing about not having money. How it makes you give up all your spare time," Lanae said.

"Unless you don't have a job, like me. Then you can use all that spare time you suddenly have to relax by worrying that you'll never be employed again," I said.

"I don't know how to get you a job," she said, "but at least we can get rid of our debt."

"Hey, I also like having an unbruised face."

"I love how you've gotten me to talk about my other self who grows plants and takes naps during the day," Lanae said. "As if I would have known what to do in college to become her. I didn't even know what college was when I got there."

"I don't know a single first-generation college student who had any idea how to draw a straight line between college and what they could do for the rest of their lives. We lacked that whole nepo baby know-what-to-do-for-the-summer-internship-because-our-moms-already-do-it thing."

"I never understood that," she said. "How your summers were supposed to build toward a job."

We sat in the car staring at nothing until six p.m., when our skinny, energetic-looking security guy was subbed out for a thicker, slower, barrel-chested Latin guy. The two guards exchanged one of those handshakes that has seven parts to it. The younger guy left.

"I like the new guy," Lanae said. "He doesn't look like he can run."

We stayed exactly where we were for another hour-plus, scared to pee. I looked away for a hot second.

"A cleaning crew," Lanae said.

Two people, a man and a woman, wore the same light blue uniform and fished large clear plastic bags out of the back of their truck.

"No more employees, huh," Lanae said.

"They must use the front door. But they're gone. I've had one office job, once, just temp work, but nobody was working by the time the cleaning crew showed up," I said.

The cleaning crew walked past the security guard, waved, and went into the building, where they stayed for forty-eight minutes before resurfacing with their clear plastic bags full of trash. They waved goodbye to the guard, disappeared into their truck, and pulled into traffic. I was ashamed that I hadn't noticed their truck the minute they parked it, since it was an enormous light blue eyesore that said TRASHED, with an illustration of a passed-out guy next to two uniformed workers picking up a trash bag that lay next to him. It didn't feel like a commentary on drunkenness or garbage. It was more confusing than that.

Our new security guy alternated between doing his laps and sitting, until 8:48 p.m., when he disappeared for thirty minutes and came back with a greasy paper sack of food and a drink with a straw in it. He ate in his chair and sat back on it when he finished, with the satisfied posture of the well fed. We watched and waited.

I silently marveled at the circumstances that had made a middle-aged, out-of-shape guy a sight we couldn't take our eyes off. At 10:03 p.m. his head drooped to one side.

"You think he's asleep?" Lanae said.

"Roll your window down. Stay quiet. He looks like a snorer," I said. "We'll hear him."

We waited one beat, two beats, three. He started snoring. Lanae rolled her window back up.

At 10:32 p.m. he sat up, stood up, and wandered away, but he came right back. We took turns peeing on the side of the car in the dark and waited for him to leave, but he didn't. We took sleeping shifts before Lanae shook me awake, just before six a.m., to watch him get replaced by the skinny guard. But she had to get to work, so I hightailed it back to Echo Park via Cesar Chavez until it turned into Sunset. Past the closed shops and the streets empty but for a single homeless encampment, a lone blue tent standing against a fake rock formation built to keep the houses on the hill on top of it from falling into the street. We'd end up doing ten more stakeouts to make sure we had everyone's building routine down, but I always remembered the first one most fondly, the one we did while shot through with ignorance, adrenaline, and hope.

"Maybe we could sneak in during the dinner break?" Lanae said, two turns away from her apartment.

"If he takes the same thirty minutes," I said. "Or we could figure out a way to replace the trash team and knock him out."

"I'm not knocking anyone out."

"Maybe it wouldn't have to come to that. We should talk to Audrey, see how much time she needs. Go back in the morning sometime to do a full day's watch and see if there's another window. I'll come down until I've nailed everyone's routine, take notes, let you guys know what I see."

"Why wouldn't we just come down here after he leaves to go get dinner at eight forty-eight p.m.?" Lanae said.

"I don't know," I said.

"Because you've been watching too many movies. We're not trying to make friends with him. We can just wait until he's gone."

"True."

"You're afraid to do this. That's why you're proposing ideas that wouldn't work," Lanae said.

"No, I'm not," I said. "I'm dying to do this."

"You're supposed to be the master thief among us and you're scared."

"I've swiped a few pieces of jewelry."

"And skimmed some credit cards. Don't sell yourself short. I was a little weirded out by the idea at first, but I was born for this. And I can't afford to get beat up at work again. I'm a punk. We throw rules in the garbage all the time. You're a small-time crook trying to upscale and feeling bad about it."

"You didn't tell me they got you at work," I said.

"They didn't hurt my face, so I figured I didn't have to say anything."

"I would still have wanted to know!"

"Maria thinks there's something wrong with me. You know her, she's very much one of those skinfolk that ain't kinfolk. Well, skinfolk really ain't kinfolk when you're getting beat at work, I guess. Audrey helped me up and sat me in the back room until our shift ended, but Maria's been giving me the eye ever since. I'm terrified to lose that job. A lot of our gigs pay in flop sweat."

"You're not gonna lose that job," I said.

Lanae sighed.

"You tell Maria that. I still have a limp, I can just hide it better now. I hate living like this. All I want is for the debt cops to leave me alone so I can go to work and play my music and leave it at that."

"You can't have that unless you get rich," I said.

"See, that's the thing that gets me about what we're doing. There isn't even any money in it. So we erase some databases. I'll appreciate that a lot. But I'm still going to end up struggling between two jobs," Lanae said.

"All the choices we have are garbage. Keep having debt and get our asses kicked, or let our loans and one more financial mistake drag us down into all the shit that happens to the poor-poor and the homeless. This at least gets the loans off our backs so we can live regular on-the-fence lives."

"I get it. Part of me just wishes, since we're going to this much trouble, that we were robbing a casino," Lanae said.

"You want money," I said.

"Cold hard cash!"

"Twenties, fifties, or hundreds."

"Whatever you have, girl!" she said.

We laughed.

I took a left and a right. In a flash, we were up the stairs, into her place, and down for, in her case, the hour and a half that remained of the night. I heard her snoring in her bedroom, but out on the couch I moved from dead tiredness to the mild internal vibrations of insomnia, aided by the sun creeping through her kitchen window.

I did think of prison, mostly as a dim, cold room where, other than not being able to leave, the worst punishment would be my own thoughts of failure. But I mostly dreamed of the other side. The version of my life where I was debt-free. Lanae wanted to be rich. If great wealth dropped into my life, so be it. But I mostly wanted to be the me I was before. If we pulled this off, I'd give myself a second chance at the life I really wanted. I'd scratch and claw my way back onto film sets. I would take the ruins of my life and shape them into something that mattered.

Fourteen

Audrey and I were hanging out in Lanae's apartment the next day, on her living room couch. Lanae was off at a gig.

"How's the building doing?" she asked me.

I summarized our day. The day guard, the night guard, the employee with a building badge he had to swipe to get in. The busyness of the block. The cleaning crew. Zapp's Cajun Hellfire chips, which had left some hellfire in the bottom of my stomach, sending me to the cold comfort of yogurt to rectify things. Audrey eyed me with suspicion. *Come on, girl!* I said to her in my head. *We're working together! Just pretend I'm a criminal you can trust!*

"And what's in their systems?" I asked her.

"I've been poking around in their shit as far as I can get. I thought some of the people in that office would work from home, like the D.C. employees. But they don't. This office seems to be the mother ship. It has thirty-five upper-level employees who oddly all report to a physical office Downtown, instead of doing their database work from home."

"What weirdos. What would anyone need to do for a loan company that would require going into an office?" I said.

"Be micromanaged. But the good news is that some CEO with visions of everyone catching up around the watercooler like it's 2015 is going to make this a lot easier. I was thinking maybe they'd spread their key employees across states. I figured we might have to break into someone's house to get into their computer system. And I'm not breaking into some white person's house."

"I'm not breaking into anybody's house. I pass so many houses around here that have signs that are like, 'Watch out, our dogs might kill you.' Sometimes it feels like the culture here is mostly building security and tacos."

"Luckily, it's pretty easy to, if you know what you're doing, just waltz into a lot of offices."

"I don't know about waltz," I said. "Real offices have security that at least makes you think. This place has two security guys who sit out back and some kind of key card that gets you in the front and back doors. They have to have indoor security, too, but I can't figure that out from my car."

"Is there anyone who doesn't use the key cards?"

"Everyone uses them, even the cleaning staff."

"How good are you at cleaning?" Audrey said.

"My old apartment was spotless, if you don't count the piles of unwashed clothes or the six-month-old flour spill in the cabinet. But I can get in with a cleaning crew."

Audrey looked unconvinced.

"What? I can be charming. How do you think I sold so many dresses?"

"I need you to get into the office to tell me what I'm dealing with. Is there a printer with a make and model name? Sometimes people connect printers to their networks, and I can get into their online system that way. Is there a security system box on the wall? If there is, and it's a smart system, I can get into their system and knock it out if we ever needed to go back in there."

"The cleaning crew tends to come by after everyone's gone home for the day, but I'll see what I can do," I said.

Audrey got up to get a glass of water from the kitchen. I lay down on Lanae's rug and felt good. We were coming up with the bones of a plan. Maybe this was possible.

"How are you going to fit in with a cleaning crew?" Audrey said, sitting back down on the couch and killing my vibe of accomplishment.

"I'll figure it out," I said.

"If we can get you in, I'll give you flash drives with a little bit of bad code on them. You can drop them on the floor. Someone will pick one up, pop it in to figure out what's on it, and bam. I'm in."

"I've picked up so many things that weren't mine off floors. I can figure out a way to drop something off."

Fifteen

In my car the next day, at 6:29 p.m., I looked up from Lanae's watch and saw the Trashed truck pull into its normal parking spot. There is never a good time to approach people doing shift work. If you go for before their shift starts, they're antsy that talking to you will make them late, and therefore possibly fired. If you roll up to them after their shift ends, they're tired from standing or walking or cleaning and they hate you for adding minutes to their journey back to their living room couch. But I didn't want to get anyone fired. So I waited the forty-eight minutes until they came back out on the street to run up to them as they loaded their truck.

"Hi," I said breathlessly.

"Hi," both the man and the woman said, after making what-are-you-doing-here eye contact with me.

"I need a job," I said, not wanting to waste a second of my time, "and I was wondering if I could come clean with you."

His face blew up into a balloon of laughter. Her face blew up into a balloon of laughter. They let out their face balloons by laughing at me. I laughed too, so I could pretend we were all part of an amazing private joke.

"Do you think we hire people?" the woman said.

"Uh . . . ," I said. "I don't know. Do you?"

"Us personally? No," she said.

"I got hired because a friend of mine worked here," the guy said.

"Me too," the woman said. "Do people ever get hired, just like, right off the street?"

"You mean, like, right off the curb where she's standing?"

"Yeah. Right there."

"I don't think so."

"You should try another curb, honey," the woman said.

They looked at me with a finality in their faces.

"Good luck," the woman said.

I stood there, completely flustered, as they drove away.

Back at Lanae's place, I internet-searched everything I could about Trashed. The only problem with internet searches is that they're garbage. I spent a couple of seconds remembering the golden days of the internet, where when you googled a term like "Trashed cleaning company," the first set of hits would involve the company you were looking for instead of sponsored ads for garbage cans. Who the hell sponsored an ad for a garbage can? Why, even if you put your phrase in quotes, did the search results pull up nothing?

Twenty internet pages later, after I sorted through my fill of sponsored garbage cans and drunk women, I finally found the company's website. Trashedcompany.com had a landing page full of people who looked so happy cleaning a room in their Trashed uniforms that it seemed like a shot from a musical.

I skimmed their mission: "to dust off the windows of our soul," and their origin story. The founders were two guys who met in college, realized after a hard night of drinking that all the guys in their college lived in filth, and started Trashed by offering to clean everyone else's dorm rooms. I shuddered, imagining them spending all those mornings many of us spent hungover cheerfully mopping up different colors of puke. The rest of their website swore that they weren't just a cleaning company, which I genuinely hoped meant they sold drugs. Instead they insisted that their company wasn't quite a family, but full of those cool cousins everyone had who could really wax a floor.

After triple-checking their website to make sure "wax a floor" wasn't a euphemism for a weird sex act, I copied and pasted the email address on their "contact us" page into an email, and sent them a note explaining that I was looking for a job. I included a note that as a person who believed cleanliness was king, my values would be a good fit for their company.

Some guy called me in ten minutes, and I was assigned to a shift two days later. Everything in life should be that easy. I mean, getting a job is easy, if you're willing to lift boxes heavy enough to break your back, drive a car for pay while rolling the dice that none of your passengers want to assault you, or give up having a lunch break or a bathroom that wasn't a bush just out of sight of a security camera. I'd scoured the Trashed website and all the online employee reviews I could find. The job couldn't be that bad, right?

Two days later, I learned to dust, mop, scrub counters, and dump garbage cans. Later that day, they sent me to a series of Downtown office buildings, where I scrubbed until my hands were sore, shined up counters until everything reeked of bleach, and dumped garbage cans until my wrists were numb. The blue uniform went from stiff to irritating to something I stripped off at the end of the day to treat the rash that rose up on my neck. I went home that first day and texted Audrey on my burner phone.

"You got the job?" she said, bursting into Lanae's place at midnight, while Lanae slept.

"Shhh," I said, hooking a thumb at Lanae's bedroom door. "You know it."

"Do you know where you're supposed to clean every day?"

"They're going to assign me a different driving route every day."

"I'm going to give you seven corrupt flash drives, like we talked about, and if you get assigned to that office, I want you to drop them in people's cubicles or under the desks in their offices."

She left and came back three hours later with the drives, right as I was about to go to sleep. The next day I tucked them in my pocket and drove to work, terrified that they would fall out.

At the Trashed office, I was assigned to a daily route, and hopped into a Trashed truck with my partner, a sweet guy named Jimz.

"The *z* is silent," he said.

"Right," I said.

We drove around to the offices on that day's route, observing all the company rules. Only enter through the back door. Avoid all employees like they're covered in ants. Never make eye contact with anyone at what the company said was a trash site and normal people would have just called an office. We were being timed, so if we spent an extra unnecessary minute inside a trash site, our phones would beep. Attached to our list of daily sites was a table that explained exactly how long it should take to clean each office. I got used to power walking around cubicles and quickly stuffing smaller trash bags into my bigger one, as if dumping trash was the anchor leg of a 4x100 meter relay.

Jimz peed into bottles. I found alley corners. We weren't allowed official breaks. We stuffed food into our mouths en route. I should have known better. The more fun and millennial the company seems, the worse the culture. If the uniforms look cute, if the website has any of that weird pink they've assigned to people in their thirties and early forties, if there is any reference to family in the materials, like "all our employees are a family," or their line about how all their employees thought of each other as cousins, or shit like that, you will need a year of therapy after the job ends.

Jimz and I went everywhere from lavish high-rise Downtown office palaces to suspiciously seventies suburban office parks, which, other than their varying sizes, all looked roughly the same. Any designer who dared suggest that an office carpet be a color that couldn't be described as tan or brown must have been beheaded. Break rooms had the same K-Cups and tea bags that I made smell like ammonia. Cubicles were spotless, or covered in crumbs, or once in a while mysteriously covered in paper. What did I learn from all that trash? Everything. While I didn't, due to the length of our shifts, have time to study what people threw away, I could make do with a casual glance. People were into yogurt cups and against sandwich crusts. They threw out untouched sheets of printer paper. A handful of weirdos shaped their garbage paper into airplanes, like they'd decided to live in seventh grade forever. People threw away stuff they should have shredded or lit on fire. If I'd known more about how corporations worked, I could have done more with the machine prototypes and legal filings that I hauled into my bigger trash bag en route to a landfill. But I didn't care about their trash. I was waiting.

Thirty-two days into the job, Jimz, on his way to the next site, made some turns onto familiar streets. I felt the high tide of hope. He parked. We grabbed our cleaning kit, waved hello to the security guard I'd watched from my car, and used our security keys to enter through the back door.

I had never, in my life, been so excited to enter an office. You'd have thought those white walls and tan carpet we found on the second floor of the building were gonna throw me a party.

The office had a standard layout. A set of cubicles that sat in its center for the worker bees, and a ring of offices that bordered the perimeter of the building for the queen bees. Jimz and I split up to cover half the office apiece. I listened to the low-level buzz all offices emitted, a combo of server noise, running refrigerators, and generic white room noise. But this office noise I would savor. All the different humming sounds had the resonance other people associate with symphonies, and I felt like their conductor simply for getting inside. I listened to the soothing sounds of Jimz wiping down counters and mopping the office's break-room floor while

I went to the cubicles to start dumping the trash. Grab, dump, replace. Grab, dump, replace. Shit, I'd gotten into rhythm and forgotten to drop my flash drives.

I grabbed a full trash bin in front of me, dumped its trash into my larger bag, and gently slid a flash drive under the cubicle it belonged to while my head was down under the cubicle, to block the view of what I was doing. One down, six to go. My ears were on. My vision sharp. The fatigue that usually set in two to three jobs into a shift swapped itself out with adrenaline, as if being in a corporate office had the same vibe as being whipped around by a roller coaster. As I'd suspected, no one in the building was working late, so it was just me, Jimz, his cleaning products, and my mission. I scanned the walls and noted the Selectrica brand security system, since Audrey had told me to. I wasn't going to have time to note its model number, but I could describe the thin teal stripe it had running down its middle.

Grab, dump, replace. I quietly slid the second flash drive under a cubicle the same way I'd slid the first one. Grab, dump, replace. Grab, dump, replace. There went number three. I threw four tiny office garbage cans of discarded food and paper into the mouth of my bag. I saw spreadsheets. I saw charts. I spotted people's loan balances, as if those needed to be printed out in our era. So much pain for whoever these pieces of paper referenced on the end of the transaction so far away from the part of it that had become someone's carelessly tossed-off garbage. Fuck these people, and the debt they hung over all our necks like an albatross. Grab, dump, replace. Grab, dump, replace. Goodbye, flash drive number four.

Jimz caught my eye to give me the halfway-done signal. I returned it. They kept every single one of these offices at a perfectly climate-controlled sixty-eight degrees, but of course, due to the drives in my pocket, I was sweating. I worked my way through the last line of cubicles and dropped a flash drive under the final one. I went into my first of ten offices. I hated offices. I could get into a rhythm with cubicles, which were faster. I could reach over and do my business in a handful of swift motions in a cubicle. Offices slowed me down. They were deep enough that I had to physically wander into them. And most office dwellers tended to keep their cans right by their office chairs. To them this represented ease and convenience, to me a doubling of the distance between me and any cubicle garbage can.

I dropped the fifth drive in the first office and the sixth one in office number five. After the excitement of dropping most of my drives, the job had turned mechanical again. I figured whenever they sent the machines to eliminate low-wage work, they'd come for this job first. A robot could reach its robot arm out and robotically dump smaller garbage bags into a bigger one, just like I did. But I smiled at the thought that a robot garbage collector, according to Audrey, if it was connected to the network, could be used to hack into the security system, just like me.

From the doorway of the seventh office, I spotted something on the floor. A tiny, rectangular, black-and-gold security key. Back in the day, I'd made friends with one of the writers at my most steady place of employment, *Star Peace*, a doomed Star Wars television reboot for people who hated the heightened conflict of the original. Somehow it took four seasons for people to get sick of gentle, virtually nonconsequential fights, even if they involved recognizable versions of the original characters and some space lasers even I, a Star Wars agnostic, had to admit looked cool. When the writer was showing me a cut of his season three episode, I noticed him authenticating himself with a username, a password, and a tiny rectangular device that looked exactly like the security key on the floor. I asked what the device was and enjoyed a brief trip to the world of very important people. It turned out television productions were just as big on secrecy as regular corporate office work, out of fear that somebody might leak episodes of a show that hadn't aired yet. So they loaded their writers up with two-factor authentication tools. The second I recognized that security key, three years of dressing people in mirror-coated vinyl space suits became the most useful job of my life.

I scooped the security key off the floor just in case Audrey could do anything with it, looked out the office window, and saw the security guard, who stood one story below me, at an angle where he might have been looking me straight in the eye. I'd turned the office lights on to grab the trash, so he might be able to see me. I tried to remember if I had, from the angle he was looking at me from outside, the cover of a tinted office window, but no luck. He scowled at me. Shit. Weaker people would have thought about putting the security key back after that, but I figured I'd let him confront me on our way out the door if he was serious. He could wrestle the security key out of my dead Black hands.

I went through office eight. Office nine. Office ten. One more garbage can that I had to grab and dump so we could get out of there. I took my usual handful of steps to the back side of the desk to approach the can. It lay in the same place as all the other office garbage cans. A crumpled sheet of paper lay next to it. I took the briefest of glances at the paper so I didn't slow down my process too much. It was a printed email about making sure everyone saved all account information to the backup server, which saved it to a physical backup hard drive. I "accidentally" knocked a tissue out of my big garbage bag on top of the paper, picked up both items, stuffed them in my pocket, and dropped my last thumb drive under the desk.

"You done?" Jimz yelled to me outside the office, in the cubicles.

"You bet," I said.

Our timing alarm beeped, as if we needed a third party to tell us to leave.

I quickly dumped the office garbage can into my larger bag.

In a blink we were back outside, my happy place, away from that office, which had turned airless the second I spotted the security guard from inside, given that he might know about the security key I'd lifted. It was fifteen steps from the back office door to our Trashed truck. Each step took three years as I looked at the guard and waited for my fate. He held our gaze for a beat too long. Would he tackle me, yank the drive out of my pocket, and call the cops? I took two shallow breaths. He nodded at us and went back to his phone. Holy shit, I was free. We jumped in the van, me with that security key and wadded-up email resting hotly in my pocket. We drove off to the next mind-numbing job.

At three a.m., after I finished my shift, I texted Audrey, told her what happened at work, and said she could come over to

Lanae's the next day to check it out. But she said she couldn't wait. While Lanae slept in her bedroom, Audrey and I sat in the living room. She held the printed-out email and the security key. I downed water after a long, dry shift at a job where I never had a spare moment to drink anything. She turned over the security key with wonder, like it would open up a fancy castle in one of those movies that was absolutely stuffed with elves.

"Amazing," she said. "Just incredible."

"You can work with this."

"Between what's on the flash drives and the security key, I'll be able to put together the rest of the hack."

"Fantastic."

"But I'm going to have to look around in their systems to figure out where the hard drive in the email is physically located. People who work in offices send too many emails. I'm sure I'll find one that tells me where they keep the drive. Also there's a chance, since they're dumb enough to make everyone important report to one physical office, that they keep the hard drive in that office too. If that's so, we're going to have to go in and get it."

"Oh please," I said. "They'll mount it outside."

"Ha," Audrey said, with a dead look on her face.

"I can't lift a hard drive at work, though. I'm going to have to quit and find another way in."

"Why?"

"They don't give us enough time on the shifts for me to root around and find anything, and I can't exactly grab a hard drive while my teammate's there."

"At least you filched the building key they gave you, right?"

"They don't let you keep anything," I said.

"That's never stopped you before."

"When we get back to the main hub after a shift, they make us hand over all the building keys."

"Oh," she said.

"If I were to try to hold on to a building key today, when I've been dropping off flash drives, it would have looked really bad. You want me to get fired some other day."

"I really hate those motherfuckers," she said.

"The cleaning company? Oh, I hate them too."

"No, the government. Not that your cleaning people sound fun, but if the government had cared that I hadn't actually slipped anyone classified info, I could have paid back my loans. But they didn't know who did it at first, and so they blamed me, fired me, and only later did they find out who was at fault."

"What got leaked?"

"I can't tell you."

"What are they gonna do? Fire you?"

"Prosecute me, actually? There's never a good time to leak confidential info, even after they fire you."

"C'mon, you might get prosecuted for what we're doing."

She sighed.

"All I'm going to say," she said, "is that someone leaked the blueprints of our gym."

"You got canned because someone knows where the NSA's weight room is? I thought leaking scandals were bigger than that. You know, like somebody leaked what's on Japan's mind today."

"That place is a fortress. Somebody went to all that effort to figure out useless shit like where we kept the towels. But when there's a leak, somebody always gets fired. And even though I didn't do it, I might not have 'fit in with the culture.' They'd never had a Black girl hacker before. On my first day there, some white girl asked me if I knew Beyoncé."

"Fuck them."

"Yeah. I want to clean out my loan debt. But I also want to aim a middle finger to the people who canned me for no reason."

"I love when they underestimate us," I said.

I didn't really care. Who could walk around with the low expectations of white people in their heads all the time? But I wanted to keep her fired up, and it worked. That was me, crime cheerleader, ready with my pom-poms and an illegal plan.

"Watch them underestimate me now," she said.

Sixteen

A week later Lanae had yet another gig, which was bizarre. Was there a sudden demand for the kind of punk music that sounded like someone had run over a bat with a lawn mower? Audrey came over so the three of us could pregame for Lanae's gig. I'd reached a truce with Lanae's music, but Audrey had become a real fan, even if she refused to dress right. She stubbornly insisted on wearing at least one other color with her black. Tonight she had on black pants and possibly the least punk shirt of all time: a fuchsia T-shirt that said SANTA MONICA FUN RUN. From extremely limited conversations with Lanae's bandmates and her other punk friends, my idea of punks was that they were the kind of people who found fun depressing. But I loved a look that would fuck with people, and Audrey had brought one.

Every time I saw someone serving, I mourned my lost wardrobe. For a couple weeks after all my stuff disappeared, I'd tried to see if I could find any of it, but the word was that people didn't get their stuff back from the debt police. Lanae lent me the outfit I was wearing for the night: a plain black T-shirt and black leggings that laced up like shoes on their sides.

Instead of my usual half-full glass of tequila, Lanae and Audrey had moved me onto cheap red wine. Tequila and I had a relationship, built off years of being broke. Every bar has some rail tequila, and I could sip that shit for hours, an act that only cost me the price of one drink. I knew about the existence of cheap wine, but I still saw wine as a drink for fancy people who liked to swirl drinks around in their glasses and talk about notes. Yet sitting on Lanae's floor sipping it forced me to conclude that red wine wasn't bad. Besides, maybe after we pulled this off, I'd feel free to become someone else, like a person who liked wine. I thought of all the cumulative time in my life that I'd spent making decisions based on how much they wouldn't send me further into debt. But here I was, inches away from a future new me, who no matter what the rest of her problems might be, at least wouldn't have the debt police at her door.

Lanae set out some chocolate.

"I hate punk-branded shit, but a friend sells this stuff, and we're all trying to help her make rent this month," she said, pointing to her kitchen table.

It was covered in chocolate bars. I picked one up.

"Chocolate Casbah," I read off the label. "Chocolate that doesn't play by the rules."

I put the chocolate bar down.

"Absolutely not," I said.

"I know," Lanae said.

"Chocolate Casbah, Chocolate Casbah," Audrey sang to the tune of the song.

"What does chocolate that doesn't play by the rules even mean?" I said.

"Maybe it's chocolate that's actually vanilla," Audrey said. "You know, edgelord chocolate."

"The woman who made this is so sweet and pure that she can't possibly have any idea what an edgelord is. This is regular chocolate," Lanae said.

"But it claims to be good in some way, right?" Audrey said.

"Not really," Lanae said. "Sometimes people just be out there selling new products, and telling you the point is that they're new."

She moved to the bathroom, left the door open, and started in on her makeup. Watching her do her makeup always felt like what I imagined it would feel like to watch an architect build a building. Just layer after layer of stuff I only vaguely understood, and then bam! A house.

She started with foundation, the painters' canvas of makeup. I knew how makeup worked in the sense that I knew what would highlight clothes, since I'd grown up with my makeup-counter-employee mother and worked with enough makeup artists to get the drift, but I'd never gotten into it for myself. Everyone I knew who really liked makeup was obsessed with facial transformation in a way that I wasn't. I liked my face. It was pointy and brown and high-foreheaded and mine. And I never wanted to ruin clothes. Even when I worked at Phoenix, and I knew it didn't matter like it mattered on film or TV sets, because no one would ever see it, I still cringed when I went to clean out a fitting room and saw a shirt marred by a smear of foundation.

But Lanae needed her makeup. To be seen properly under the lights. To give off the right look. She finished her foundation and went for powder, then eye shadow.

"Do you all ever worry about getting old?" she said.

"Aren't we already old, by female standards?" Audrey said. "Don't all women die at thirty?"

"I will never worry about getting old," I said. "I worry about accidentally drifting into that stage of life where you give up and start shopping at whatever the cheaper version of Eileen Fisher is, because life is too short to ever own shirts that are so big and shapeless that it looks like you're trying to hide an entire Monopoly board under them. But I don't worry about getting old. Old is still an age that can be rocked. Naomi Campbell. Tina Turner. Helen Mirren."

"You don't really believe that," Lanae said.

"I do. Old is a slightly different, but still stunning wardrobe."

"You're not worried that opportunities are foreclosed to you?" Audrey said.

"Like what, having a good job?" I said. "I have a great job. I eat food on camera for a bunch of guys who don't really pay me."

I'd quit Trashed via email that morning, to make sure enough time had passed since I'd lifted the security key to seem unsuspicious. To celebrate, Lanae drove me to the grocery store before her shift, where I'd used some Trashed cash to buy walnuts, green beans, jarred tomato sauce, and two pounds of spaghetti I could seductively slurp into Lanae's laptop camera. I'd put up a message on my site and all my social media about how I was just coming back from a very refreshing spring break, which they'd picture as me sunning myself on a beach somewhere instead of peeing into bushes while Jimz yelled at me to hurry up and get back in the truck. Until we pulled this off, I would happily return to work, thrilled that it didn't involve trash sites, timers, or coworkers who were just like family.

"Or a better job than that?" Audrey said.

"Or stuff like travel," Lanae said.

"Or what next, kids? A house with a picket fence? Other dreams of the past that I'll never be able to afford? As much as I try not to think about it, when I'm not worrying about money, I worry about ending up lying across the backseat of my car spitting blood on a parking space again. It's hard for me to think of the future when I spend all my time running from the present," I said.

"I'm still trying to think about the future," Audrey said. "When I see one of those turquoise cars on the street, I just try not to imagine the version of the future where it follows me for a couple of miles before kicking my ass again."

"I worry about getting old. I see the younger punk girls out there and they look less resigned. I think that's what I lost when they beat me up. Before that I was working and doing shows and feeling like I was at the center of something. And now I feel like a stranger breaking into my own life," Lanae said.

"Now you get to break into a building and get away with that instead," I said.

"If we don't just go to prison. We're Black girls. A lot of us end up in prison."

"I'm worried too, but this kind of hack is hard to trace," Audrey said.

"What about the hard drive?" Lanae asked.

We'd filled her in on what we'd figured out about the job so far.

"What about it?" I asked.

"We've gotta go in there for that."

"Don't worry about it. I'm gonna slide in there like a pat of butter in a cut potato," I said.

"But what am I going to do?" Lanae asked.

"You're going to distract the guard, because you have more of a distracting-men look than I do," I said. "If you've ever looked into World War II, you're going to be our honeypot trap. But you don't have to kill him, unless that's your thing."

"You're the pretty one," Audrey said. "You can do it. I'll knock out the indoor security, but we have to take the outside guard out of the equation."

I knew I wasn't the pretty one in virtually all the groups of girls I'd ever been in, but I won't lie. It still stung to hear that somebody else got that bag. Even though Lanae deserved it. She had a delicate face, like a deer, and the men at her shows always packed the front row, trying to see if they could get close enough to touch her.

"You guys don't seriously mean kill him?" Lanae asked, with her hand shaking as she applied eyeliner to her left eye. She stopped, blotted it off, and tried again.

"No, I don't mean kill him. Throw him off," I said.

"How?"

"You distract men a few nights a week," I said. "You're a natural.

You'll figure it out. That way you don't have to go into the building, or do the hack. You're lifting the lightest load. You can do your thing and get right back in the car if you want. I can take care of the drive."

"Really?" Lanae asked.

"Yeah," Audrey and I said.

"Okay."

"Phew," I said.

"Don't worry, I wasn't wussing out."

"I wasn't worrying," I said, putting an extra degree of calm into my voice to sell the lie.

I could see her wussing out. Calculating how much prison she could avoid by telling the debt cops what we did. I also imagined the version of her that figured out how to distract the guard and went running down that alley to somewhere where I'd never see her again. That was the worst part of all this. The vibe that I couldn't trust them.

Despite being a punk, Lanae was secretly the most conventional of us. She didn't seem to burn for revenge in the same way that Audrey and I did. Audrey and I were furious about what we'd suffered through, but Lanae mostly seemed tired. I'd been friends with her longer than Audrey, but every time I really thought about what we would be doing, I pictured her as the one who might figure out how to flake off. She always seemed to be off at a show when Audrey and I were plotting. She had ambition in the rest of her life. Me and Audrey had nothing going on. Lanae could cop out on us on a whim for her band. But there weren't a whole lot of wildly successful thirty-eight-year-old Black female musicians, and she didn't give off signs of thinking that if she sold us out she could make herself the exception.

"I read somewhere that the German word for debt means guilt," Lanae said, "but why should I feel guilty for being working class?"

There's my girl. Get angry, Lanae. She moved her eyeliner pen over to her right eye. I took a good look at her and felt sad that she was looking a little older lately. The thing about friends is that they should remain young and unafraid and immortal. But we would all turn forty soon enough, and our late thirties felt like a sledgehammer. We weren't young and full of potential anymore. We were older, and we hadn't paid our debts.

Audrey sometimes told a story about competing in a high school track meet. She went to the only high school in her division that made people compete on concrete instead of rubber. She would rush ahead only to be tortured by the sound of everyone else's steps thundering behind her like a pack of horses. When I thought about my loan balance, I could hear the sounds of her concrete track.

"So when are we going to talk over the plan?" Audrey asked.

"Whenever," I said.

"Not now," Lanae said. "Not right before a gig."

"We're all here," Audrey said.

"C'mon, Lanae," I said. "You've still got eighty-seven layers of makeup to go, right? You have time to hear the plan."

"If you absolutely need to talk about this now, fine. I can't like, look at a map or anything, because I have to keep doing my makeup," she said, putting on eye shadow. "There's no map, right?"

"No, this isn't one of those stories with snowfall and elves and a pilgrimage to the north," I said.

"So I invented a program called Paid in Full," Audrey said.

"We all wish," Lanae said.

She finished up her eye shadow and started in on her cheek bronzer.

"It mimics their antivirus software. Their system is set up to automatically update their antivirus program, and the next time it'll do that is Sunday, May eleventh."

"So that's our night," I said.

"Yup," Audrey said. "But instead of running a normal update, it's going to run the zero-day program that I invented after hanging out in their code. It'll write over all the loan balances in its system with the words 'paid in full.'"

"What's a zero-day program?" Lanae asked.

"A virus that, when they find it, they have zero days to fix, because it's going to fuck their systems up seven ways to Sunday," Audrey said. "The virus will crawl into their systems at eight forty-nine p.m., which is when they normally do their system updates. It'll take ten minutes to fully do its thing. In addition to erasing everyone's loan balances, it'll knock out their building security and the lights. Since the building security will be out, we should be able to just open the back door without a key. That's when Jada's going to take the hard drive."

"Right at nine," I said.

"So it'll be dark," Lanae said.

"That's okay," I said. "We'll bring flashlights if we need them, but I work just fine in the dark. There's street light too. If the guard is there for some reason, instead of on break, we're going to knock him out and go in. If he shows up while we're there, we'll knock him out and leave."

"I'm not punching anybody," she said.

"No, you're not. He comes back with his food right before nine thirty. But we'll be gone by then. He always orders a large soda to go with whatever he's eating and sets it down next to his folding chair. If for some reason he's there when we get there, you'll distract him. I'll go in, grab the drive, and run back out. If he's there when I'm ready to leave, I'll text you and Audrey on the burner, and you'll come distract him so I can get out."

"How am I going to distract him?" Lanae said.

"You'll flirt with him. Right when it looks like you've hooked him, I'll make some noise. When he gets up to check it out, you're going to roofie his drink."

Lanae gasped, lipstick in hand.

"No," she said.

"Yes," I said.

"Wow," she said. "I have friends who've been roofied, and it's a rough couple of days. Week if you get unlucky."

"He's gonna be fine. He's gonna sleep for four to six hours, which will leave him plenty of time to forget who we are and wake up before he has to switch shifts with the day guard. Again, you're not gonna kill him."

"I sure as hell hope not," she said.

"I'm going to get roofies for you, crush 'em up, and put them in a little plastic bag. You're going to open the bag up and dump it in his drink. He always drinks out of one of those gas station Styrofoam cups," I said.

"Okay," Lanae said nervously.

"He'll pass out. We'll drive away," I said.

"That sounds straightforward," Lanae said. "But would you ever need me to go in?"

"If anything seems wrong inside the building, I'll tap the back window. The guard will be passed out, so it'll be easy for you to pop inside to serve as the lookout so I can grab the drive. But nothing's gonna go wrong."

"You two are key," Audrey said. "Their systems have to be wrecked with no chance of recovery, and that means destroying the hard drive. I can wreck their systems and cloud with my virus, but if they have a physical backup, the hack is worthless."

"We're on it," I said.

"Call us Missy and Timbaland," Lanae said.

"Big Meech and Larry Hoover," I said.

"Bonnie and . . . Bonnie?" Lanae said.

"Not caught," Audrey said.

"Deal," we all said.

In just four weeks, our debts would be gone forever.

Seventeen

The first three weeks went by at the speed of molasses dripping off a spoon. There were times, when I turned on Lanae's computer and placed a bowl of food in front of it to eat for money, where I felt trapped in individual minutes for at least an hour. After a long, cool winter, spring was coming in hot. Even sweating felt pointless because I wasn't in an office building lifting a hard drive.

The only thing that entertained me between downing pounds of spaghetti, eggplant, roasted almonds, and a particularly crunchy watermelon cucumber salad was designing our heist uniforms. Audrey and Lanae insisted they could just grab some nondescript black clothes from their closets, but I refused to let us proceed without a signature look. After they gave in, Audrey and Lanae pitched in to buy me an old Singer sewing machine off the internet, and I trawled the garment district just east of Downtown for the right fabrics. A month of picking through Lanae's closets had made me sick of black clothes until I held the first feasible bolt of cloth in my hand. This wasn't going to be a boring black outfit. These clothes were part of the plan that would fix my life.

I chose a flexible black jersey for the main bodysuits and their matching masks. Audrey popped over one night to get measured, as opposed to all the other nights when she popped over for no reason. I lost track of what she and Lanae were saying in the kitchen while I sewed the suits together. I'd always admired the Catwomen: Eartha Kitt, Halle Berry, Anne Hathaway, even the burned-out woman I'd worked with in *Catwoman: Cougar's Revenge*. They had tough-as-hell attitudes and those unforgettable catsuits. My black jersey fabric let me work along the lines of Hathaway's sleek, minimalist outfit in *The Dark Knight Rises*. Our suits were body-hugging numbers that covered us from the top of our necks to the tips of our toes. They had wide but flat pockets that would fit the hard drive. We'd wear them with gloves, which I'd also designed myself from the same black jersey, but with textured silicone pads that would let us operate electronics if we had to. Even though Audrey's job was to stay behind the wheel of the car while Lanae distracted the guard and I went inside, I sewed her a suit anyway.

In the kitchen, Lanae was talking about the punk documentaries she liked to watch. Most of them were in black and white with dull, grainy shots of people packed into clubs like breadsticks in a straw basket. Audrey was countering, with, of all things, action movies, which I wouldn't have thought she could have possibly been into. I remembered and then discarded the days when I only knew her as a dull retail associate, all running-girl ponytail and clothes-folding disdain.

I put them both out of my mind and focused on the point of what I was doing. The fabric slid smoothly past my hands on its way into the sewing machine to come out as a better-put-together version of itself on the other side. I'd never get over how four pieces of fabric, which unattached would be trash, transformed themselves into a bodysuit thanks to a plan and a slim line of stitching. I hadn't sewn anything since film school, when everyone else despaired over not having enough money to live in New York, and I saved cash by living off-campus with my two other Brooklyn-native roommates.

We had a lifestyle. The three of us knew the good cheap bars, and the other two tipped me a little bit to keep us all in clothes that looked better than all the supervillain fast fashion everyone else had given in to, which combined being cheap and exploitative with looking dated in three months. Even though I was too broke to buy nice clothes, I hated reading about teenagers earning a dollar in Southeast Asia for sixteen-hour shifts sewing together shirts that would fall apart three wears in. So I thrifted and I sewed, and sitting in front of that sewing machine in Lanae's living room, I remembered.

Hello to the clothes I made back in those days, from flashier, more sequined jumpsuits than I was sewing now to pastel dresses with full A-line skirts, to smoking pants and matching jackets when we felt a retro look coming on. But also hello to the motions of sewing. The rhythm. Feeding fabric into the machine. Checking that stitches had come out right. Picking apart bad stitches with a seam ripper. Getting pinched when the pins I used to stick unsewn fabric together poked me in the finger. Some people never forgot how to ride a bike, and I hadn't forgotten how to spin fabric into gold.

When the costumes were finally done, and we'd tried them on with their matching masks and admired ourselves, it was the night before our heist. As usual, we were sitting around in Lanae's living room. But unlike most nights, we'd gone sober and ordered Thai.

"Let's run through it," Audrey said. "It's nine p.m."

"I'm getting out of the car," I said.

"I'm getting out too, with one hand on the roofies in my pocket, ready for action, since I might need them on the way out," Lanae said.

"Audrey's gonna cut all the security, so the back door will be open," I said. "We pass the empty security guard chair, since he'll be grabbing dinner."

"I go in and up to the second floor. Audrey found the hard drive in office number ten, which is the last office on the right-hand row of offices, facing the back of the building and the security guard spot. I grab it and look outside. If the security guard is there before I grab the drive, I sneak around to the far end of the alley to find something to make noise with, Lanae roofies him, he passes out, I grab the hard drive, and we leave. If the guard is there after I grab the drive, I text you and Audrey, you come roofie him, he passes out, and we leave. If he isn't there, we just leave."

"I'm hanging out in front of the security guard if he's there, trying to look hot," Lanae said, getting up and doing her best hands-on-hips, fake-pout version of trying to look hot. "I'm obviously succeeding."

Me and Audrey laughed.

"Right when I reach peak hotness, Jada knocks over a trash can or something and I slip the roofie into his soda," Lanae said.

"The guard comes down the alley to see what I'm doing, but I run around the front of the building faster than he can chase me," I said.

"You guys get in and I hit the gas," Audrey said.

"To Bear Divide," I said. "Forty miles north of the city, outside Santa Clarita. We have to burn the hard drive. It's a park, but the road up to the main parking lot is gravel, and it's open all night. We can light it on fire there without anyone else seeing the smoke."

"That's it," Audrey said.

"What happens if we fuck up?" Lanae said.

"We take off. Audrey's going to be waiting out front either way," I said.

Lanae picked at her pad Thai.

"Nervous?" I asked her.

Audrey looked at her with a coolness. I eyed Audrey as if glancing at her would tell me what she was thinking, but I'd failed to figure out how to read minds with a look.

"No," Lanae said, "I'm not nervous."

We went back to our food. Audrey slurped her way through soup, and I looked down at my red curry as if I needed to document it for science instead of eat it. What I would miss if shit went wrong tomorrow was the act of hanging out with the two of them. I couldn't imagine a world where if we fucked this up, we wouldn't all go hide in separate places. I felt down when I pictured a future where I didn't know them anymore. Before I'd moved in with Lanae, I'd spent ten solid years living by myself in a successively shittier set of apartments that I loved for their solitude.

Now I liked having friends. The three of us had started spending time together to commiserate about the debt police, and then to plan the heist, but we also just hung out for no reason. I'd miss sharing a huge bowl of popcorn underneath all of Lanae's punk posters while we watched bad romantic comedies on gigless nights, or bad action movies, or the occasional good movie. Yeah, Lanae dragged us through socialist documentaries, and Audrey the entire *Fast & Furious* series, but I got used to what they put on. When it was my turn, I took them through blaxploitation. I loved the dusty-looking seventies lighting. The big soap-opera-like plot twists. And the clothes. The wide seventies suit lapels. The tiny, swingy dresses. The colors. All that mustard yellow and denim blue. The loud paisley prints. The houndstooths. The general sense that even if it was only in those movies, Black people could fuck up and get away with it.

I'd miss the bar nights where we ordered the cheapest thing on the menu and stretched it for enough time to feel like we'd had an epic night out. I'd miss the conversations and the camaraderie and the planning and the joy of sharing uncertainty and dread with other people instead of taking those feelings on alone.

If this didn't work out, I was torn between Mexico and another, cheaper town in California. I figured I could pick after I got in my car with all the nothing I owned. I'd borrowed Lanae's laptop to eat for pay, and her clothes, but my only possessions were my one athleisure outfit I was wearing when the debt cops took all my stuff, and my heist outfit, which I'd have to throw away.

Inside I was not a person of chill, but on the outside, I was ready, for the first time in my life, to look like I had never given a shit. On the street everyone had started wearing nineties trends again, and even though I wasn't a fan of spaghetti-strap dresses or Doc Martens or nostalgia, their clothes looked so much fresher and newer than the stuff we'd beaten up to get the right grunge look the first time around. I was attracted to that newness. Other than the grunge revivalists, and the always timeless LA goths, I'd surprised myself by thinking fondly of athleisure, a look I'd once associated with people willing to look awkward in spandex for entire swaths of their lives that didn't take place in a gym. I'd been with my athleisure for months. We'd stuck out our initial misgivings about each other and relaxed into quiet, stretchy companionship. If athleisure was done right, it could signal that the person wearing it didn't give a shit about style, or really much of anything. I operated on a higher frequency than people who had truly stopped caring, but I could see a future, within my reach, where I was as relaxed as my clothes looked. And tomorrow, after we burned that hard drive, I could have that future.

Eighteen

At eight p.m. on May 11, I started the most common type of car in the state of California. Lanae sat next to me. I drove with my gloves on, enjoying the feel of their silicone pads against the wheel. The sun had just gone down, and I loved the color black for once in the form of a sky that was growing dark enough to hide us. Lanae rolled her window down, so I did too, and we drove in silence, with the only sound in the car the wind whipping around her wig, since I didn't have enough Afro to whip. I retraced all my familiar turns around Downtown on our way to Audrey's place. I pulled into the right alley and saw Audrey, dressed in her heist gear with a laptop bag over her shoulder.

I drove the most common type of car in the state of California west to our destination, which, given the hour, was a dead zone slightly south of the diamond district. I pulled up to the parking spot, which left us two car lengths out of sight of the building.

"The guard's there," Lanae said.

He was sitting in his chair like it was just another night, with a bag of food and a drink sitting on the ground next to him. It was eight forty-five p.m.

"We have a plan for this," I said.

Audrey pulled out her laptop, turned it on, and logged in to the building's Wi-Fi.

"Here we go," she said.

Lanae and I watched. It was 8:49 p.m. The virus was beautiful. It truly did look exactly like the most benign thing ever, a Windows update. Once I drove back down PCH, taco in hand, to look at the stars over the darkness of the unlit beach. I remember slowing down, edging over to the side of the road, and hearing the gravel of the shoulder more than seeing it. I got out of the car to be alone with the stars, which hung gently above me, like a stylish bed canopy. I spent the first couple minutes trying to identify constellations, and found a dipper and a belt before I gave up looking for an organizing principle and leaned into enjoying how the brightness of the stars clashed with the flat black walls that led up to the sky. I hung out there for a good fifteen minutes, just me and infinity, while the very occasional car came smoking down the highway from Point Mugu, its headlights burning into me with the intensity of one of those laser pointers for cats.

Watching Audrey's virus run was like being out there in the darkness again, impressed by the calm that set in after whittling the world down to its essence. We watched her virus eat the website. It ran through files from drive to drive just like a regular update, except that instead of the regular message at the end that said the updates were complete, the site repeated the phrase "PAID IN FULL" over and over again. Then the program came to its end. She'd done it. She looked at us with a smile so big it threatened to split her face.

"Holy fucking shit," I said.

"Go," Audrey said.

We both left the car.

Nine p.m.

I slipped my mask on and crossed the street to take the long way around the block to the garbage cans.

Lanae approached the guard.

I did my block loop and slid into a carport two buildings down from the guard, looking for a good garbage can to push over, since the cans weren't where they usually were. Where the fuck were they? I walked around the cars, looking for them and keeping an eye out for other security cameras that had popped up since my last search of the area, but didn't see any. The car owner had left a toolbox on the floor of their carport, next to a black sedan. I waited a few minutes to give Lanae the chance to pretend to hit on the guard, forced the toolbox open, and started throwing wrenches in the direction of the two of them.

"Just a moment, lady," the guard said to Lanae.

He took off running.

I slipped out of the carport and sprinted around the other end of the block.

The guard went with me.

I pulled away from him on our sprint around the block and opened the security-free back door to let myself in.

Lanae followed me inside and shut the door behind us.

"You want to be the lookout," I whispered.

"Yeah," she said. "We're a team."

We climbed the stairs.

Up on the second floor, the office looked just as dark and quiet as it had been when I came to clean it. It was still just a few rows of cubicles and the offices that ringed them, but several layers of hum had disappeared. Audrey had knocked out more than just the security. I heard the loud silence of nervousness, which is a dull scream right into the ear.

"Did you do it?" I whispered to Lanae.

"Yeah, I dropped most of it in his cup," she whispered back.

"Only most of it?"

"Maybe half of it? I heard you guys coming around the corner and figured I'd better hurry up. But we're still good."

"Let's hope so. You stay here. I'll hit number ten."

"Okay."

I eased my way past the row of offices to the right of the front door, working my way through the terror of wandering in the dark through an office where I wasn't supposed to be. I noted every shadow, every corner, every square inch of that dull-ass tan carpet as if I'd be quizzed on all of it later.

I crept past the first office. The second. The third.

The office was silent and abandoned. I pictured the workers, happily going out to dinner at the sorts of restaurants whose prices made me nervous for existing, while I walked past their shut-off computers in search of something more meaningful than a twenty-five-dollar entrée.

I walked past the fourth office. For a second, I thought I heard footsteps, but when I walked down past the fifth office, where it sounded like they'd been coming from, I saw nothing.

Were there more footsteps? I snuck between a pair of cubicles to check another angle of the office. Lanae had the rest covered, and she gave me a thumbs-up. I walked down to the . . .

Behind me the footsteps were really loud.

"Jada!" Lanae yelled.

Before I could turn, or run, something came down hard on my left shoulder, from the direction of the cubicles, which was bizarre, since I'd just looked there. From the floor I looked up to see a grinning white debt cop in the first all-turquoise uniform I'd ever seen any of them wear. All turquoise. This was one hard-core motherfucker who had taken everybody's money. This was our fault, for not finding a way to completely survey the inside of the building. I don't know how we would have done that, but lying down there, with pain zinging through my shoulder, I knew that we should have figured it out.

"You don't think you're the first one to try this, do you?" he said.

I said nothing, because there's no point in talking to cops. How had we missed this guy? I'd sat in my car outside both the front and the back of the building for weeks and never saw a single debt cop come or go.

"We knew you and your gang were coming tonight, so I set up here," he said.

Gang? We were three boring women in our late thirties.

"I'm gonna call in a few of my buddies, and then you're never gonna see daylight again."

How the fuck did he know we would be there?

I tried to get up, but he hit me again. I figured I had one kick before he hurt me too badly that I'd have trouble moving, so I went for his balls with everything I had.

I got there.

He hit the floor like a picture frame in the middle of an earthquake.

If he was going to make it between him and me, I wasn't going to lose. He wasn't going to kick back with his buddies over a pedicure and some hard kombucha, talking about how crystals cure cancer and casually sliding in the story of how he kicked that wardrobe chick's ass.

I stomped on his balls. He screamed.

I kicked him in the legs.

In the arms.

Every time I kicked him, I saw everything he and his motherfucking people had done to us. Me, in the grocery store parking lot, spitting out blood. Audrey's bruised cheek and extra door locks. Lanae getting kicked out of work because black eyes don't give off the right vibes to sell clothes. The bruised Black women walking up Hillhurst. Christopher getting his ass kicked in the middle of his husband's funeral.

Everybody I'd ever met whose debt had kept them from buying a house, or being able to afford rent. Or forced them to take a job where they had to sell out everything they believed in just to make sure they wouldn't get the phone calls, or the letters, or the visits from people who might go on and on about how the power of deep tissue massage helped them find peace after knocking your jaw into the sun. My glorious clothes were sitting in a police station somewhere, surrounding people who couldn't possibly care less about them. Fuck this guy. Fuck his turquoise-costumed buddies. Fuck the student loan system. Never again.

But every kick also reminded me that I was doing my job. Lanae and I had made it here. We were on our way to destroying so much of the student debt in people's lives. I wasn't sure that I would ever have this kind of energy running through my body again. I had to keep telling myself to focus. My body felt like it could power a monster truck.

I looked around the debt cop's holster for his gun, and found it sitting far back enough that he couldn't quickly un-fetal-position himself to go get it. I kicked him in the head twice to make sure, and disarmed him.

I pointed his gun at his head.

Lanae came running down the hallway, masked. She leaned over him, opened his mouth, and forced the rest of the roofies down his throat.

He coughed and sputtered.

I expected him to spit. Why the hell wouldn't he spit? If someone put something in my mouth, I would spit it out.

He gurgled.

He passed out.

Thank god for idiots.

I searched his pockets for his phone, turned it off, and stomped on it until it broke into pieces. Lanae kicked him on his chest, arms, and legs.

"Motherfucker," she said.

Even though he was passed out, she stomped on his balls one more time.

He was debt police. We could never hurt them enough.

In my head I saw the Black cop who'd kicked my ass in that grocery store parking lot. *Look at me,* I said to him. *I'm making the right choices.*

I ran into office number ten, found the hard drive, and slid it into my pocket. I ran back out to get Lanae and saw the officer passed out on the floor, snoring.

"Let's go," I told her.

"We can't go out the door we came in," she said. "The guard's awake, looking for us."

"How do you know?" I said.

"I saw him out the window, pacing, talking on his phone."

"I thought roofies worked!"

"They usually do!"

"We gotta hit the front door then. We're gonna have to run for it."

"Oh my god," she said.

"Don't worry about it. Don't freeze up."

"Let's go."

I put the cop's gun down. We took off. Lanae pushed the door open and we went for the hardest run of our lives. Out the door, to the right, past the security guard, who barely had time to whip his head around at us, down two parking spots to the car. Lanae jumped back in the passenger seat. I was ready to take the backseat, except Audrey wasn't there.

She'd fucked us.

She'd taken her computer.

She'd left the keys on the driver's seat, but we lost enough time realizing that she'd screwed us over that the security guard was able to frantically bang on my driver's-side window.

"What the fuck do we do?" Lanae said.

The security guard reached for something.

"We drive," I said.

I flipped the car on, reversed it, and hit drive hard enough to run over the guard's feet. He took off after us anyway, limping his way down the street as fast as he could, but I made an illegal left turn down a one-way street going the wrong way.

"Watch out!" Lanae yelled.

I dodged a sedan, an SUV, a light-duty truck.

I turned onto another one-way street going the wrong way.

"Why are you going the wrong way again?" she yelled.

I pushed the car, fast. I dodged two sedans and played chicken with a third, which was too close to the other two, before swerving away at the last minute.

I pulled onto a street going the right way.

"Why would she do this to us?" Lanae said.

"Because she's never liked me," I said. "She thinks I'm a thief, and a loser. Like hackers aren't thieves. But she used to be more important than me, so she'll always be better than me."

"She's down in the shit with us," Lanae said.

"Like that's ever stopped anyone from copping out."

"I'm sorry I ever defended her to you."

"That's over now."

Audrey was gone. She could fuck us over whenever she wanted, but Lanae and I still had one more thing to do. I drove us through dark, abandoned Downtown and went through streets until I made it to the 110.

From the 110 I took the 5 north through Echo Park, Silver Lake, Los Feliz.

"She's gonna sell us out," I said.

I pushed the car to ninety.

"Please, god, I hope not," Lanae said.

Glendale popped up to our right, with its train tracks nearby, its factories and apartments behind them, and its mountains in the distance. We fled north. The buildings grew farther apart. The buildings disappeared. The hard drive felt hot in my pocket, like it might spring itself out of there and light the car on fire. We had run the virus and lifted the hard drive. This was supposed to feel great. Like a kids' birthday party, but for adults. I was supposed to feel like someone had just whipped out the Funfetti cake and handed me a big slice. And I would have but for Audrey. Thanks to her ass, I could not have the adrenaline I deserved for a job well done without a hearty dose of terror.

"We fucking did it," I said, trying to feel tougher.

Lanae howled.

I howled.

Our howling felt like it could crack the car. It drove out thoughts of Audrey and returned the night to what it should have been. A celebration of what we'd done.

I drove.

The suburban lights spread out and faded away, until we were down to highway lights.

I made the turnoff for Lancaster.

We passed through Santa Clarita and took an exit out of town.

I turned on my brights and drove into the mountains. We were the only car on the road as we went up and down hills and through switchbacks until the entrance to Bear Divide.

I stopped the car. We both got out.

I grabbed the gasoline that we'd put in the trunk.

Lanae took a box of wooden matches out of her pocket.

The bird-watchers might come to this spot for the birds, but I just needed a dirt and gravel parking lot outside the city.

I walked away from the car to put the hard drive down and pour gasoline on it. Lanae flung a lit match on top, and we ran back to stand on a lip of gravel between two dark mountain ranges and watch it burn.

"Fuck the system that put us all in this debt," Lanae said.

"Fuck the people who just made up these numbers and chained us to them."

"Fucking two-bit gangsters with their little financial aid applications," Lanae said.

"Fuck every single piece of shit that didn't give my clothes back," I said.

"Fuck the debt police," Lanae said.

"Fuck Audrey," I said.

We did it.

They were going to find us.

They might even fix the hack.

We watched the hard drive flame out and start smoking. I poured a second round of gasoline on it. Lanae lit another match. The second round of fire ate it down to a set of charred, smoking bones.

Until they found us and erased what we'd done, I could figure out what to do with the rest of my life.

But not tonight.

In the distance, I could see Richard floating in the air, in the kind of eighties power suit he'd designed himself. He was looking down at me benevolently, as if in death he'd gotten the best of both worlds. The one where he was newly debt-free, like us, and the one where it was still the eighties. Yeah, he might have sold me out, but part of me would always love him anyway.

"Richard," I whispered under my breath. "We did it."

Epilogue

They got me first, two months later. I was still crashing with Lanae and giddily checking my student loan balance, which remained at zero, until I could nail down the kind of entertainment or personal stylist job that would let me move out. During the day, while Lanae was at work, I texted people I knew and tried to convince them to give me jobs. I watched the slowly tapering-down coverage of the miserable loan company officers, who hadn't figured out how to put their systems back together. The newly debt-free had weeks of celebratory marches in the streets. It was intense, flipping on the set to watch ecstatic people talk about all the things the disappearance of their debt would let them do. And to know that I had done them that favor.

At night, when Lanae was at her gigs, I drank tequila and wondered when I'd land that next job. Sometimes I'd slip up and look in her food cabinets, imagining all the noises her food made. But Lanae said that since our debt was gone, I could take a break from chipping in on the rent and relax, an idea as alien to me as giving up on fashion.

On the morning they found me, someone knocked on the apartment door at ten thirty a.m. Eight miles away, right outside the Phoenix back door, Lanae was crying her mascara off as she was loaded into a squad car. In thirty-two minutes, they would catch Audrey at home on her day off, in the middle of her favorite post-run routine: yogurt and *The Price Is Right*.

"LA Water and Power," someone called out.

I sighed, turned off a crappy reality show about people trying to be foot models called *None of Toe Business*, slipped my house flip-flops on, tied my robe, and answered the door to two debt cops decked out in full turquoise.

"We have a warrant to take you into the station," the taller one said. In my head, I was fleeing the security guard, and disrespecting one-way streets. On the drive, I noticed that he had a manicure that was better than any I'd ever done for myself. The shorter one had set a world record for the amount of product it was possible to put in one's hair. Whenever he turned his head to talk to his buddy, I couldn't stop staring at the point he'd shaped the front of his hair into, as if it were 2005 and white men were supposed to look like their heads might spout water. Every time "Age of Aquarius" stopped playing, his taller partner put it back on. We went through fifteen excruciating minutes of conversation about darkness retreats.

"It costs two thousand dollars to go, but the upside is that you get to sit in the dark for four days," the taller one said.

"Alone?" the shorter one said.

"Completely alone. I thought so hard I was sure I could see the inside of my mind," the taller one said.

"What happens at the end? Do they just turn the lights back on?" I asked them.

"No, you have to adjust."

"Why do you guys do all the wellness stuff?"

"We were all indebted once, like you. When we satisfied our debts and joined the force, we began pursuing personal purification."

"Oh," I said, underwhelmed.

"You know," the other cop said, "if you stop buying avocado toast, you'll be able to afford a house. The only thing that really satisfies one's debts, other than money, is positive thinking and a healthy diet."

"A generous selection of crystals doesn't hurt," his partner chimed in unhelpfully.

What if, instead of listening to a single additional word of this shit, I threw myself out of the car and peacefully rolled myself under another car?

"Back to the darkness retreat," the first cop said. "You were saying."

"So over the course of a day, an attendant opens the door to your cabin one inch per hour until your body has a chance to relax, which they call full reflection. When you've fully reflected, you can enjoy a lovely meal of fruit that's fallen from the trees and fresh spring water, and then you can go home, completely purified."

"Why does the fruit have to have fallen from the trees?" said the shorter one.

"Because picking fruit is violence."

Man, I hated these guys.

We arrived at the station, where I immediately asked to speak to a lawyer, and they refused to let me call one. I know, I know, people are supposed to have rights. Not Black women, though. No one's into giving us rights we don't snatch out of their hands, and I wasn't doing any snatching in a police station. I'm sure they figured I would suddenly become suicidal or some shit after they beat me up one more time and they could be rid of me. I remembered Sandra Bland. They booked me in, took my only possession, the keys that I had to Lanae's apartment, and led me to a room.

I sat in the interrogation chair, waiting for my usual fear to bubble up into a boil. Instead, I looked at them and their uniforms and felt nothing but contempt. I had to work my ass off to keep my head above water, while they got raises and promotions for stealing other people's money. I had no inclination to talk, and I wouldn't pretend otherwise. But it was so much more satisfying to keep my answers to asking for the lawyer they didn't give me.

After a couple of hours, the tall one slammed his fists into the table that sat in front of me, and the short one rammed his head into a wall. They left, and I prepared myself for my trip to jail. This was always something that could happen, I told myself. Even though I hadn't said anything, they formally arrested me, and charged me, and left me in a single cell for two days, where I drank water and picked at shitty prison food, and tried not to think about ever getting free again. But on the third day, a guard told me someone had made my bail, and I was free to go. They handed me my clothes and gave me over to a strange clean-shaven thirtyish white guy in a black suit who reminded me of the banker bros of NYC. My banker bro led me to his beamer, and we drove away in temperature-controlled silence. This was not how being accused of a crime was supposed to work. I was supposed to be in a cell, sizing other prisoners up, coming to terms with what I'd done. Not in a car with a guy who looked like he might turn down his classical music at any moment to quiz me about tech stocks.

"Where are we going?" I said.

"I can't tell you," he said.

"You're not fucking kidnapping me, are you?"

"No, I'm not. I'm part of the group that's bailing you out."

He didn't elaborate further.

He drove me south, through Atwater and onto the 5, which we took until we left the 10 and found a house in West Adams. An expansive ranch decked out in coral-colored stucco and teal trim.

"Here you go," he said.

"Who are you? What group are you with?"

"I'm part of a group that's responsible for bringing you to this safe house. We're going to leave you alone so you can rest. Go inside and pick a bedroom. Your friends will be here soon," he said.

He drove away.

I stepped out of the car and cringed at the house's teal trim, since it looked too much like debt-cop turquoise. I looked down at my robe and flip-flops and cursed myself for not bothering to get dressed, as if I could have anticipated getting arrested that morning. I tried the front gate, and finding it open, walked up to the front door. I rang the doorbell before I noticed the note taped to the door, which told me the combination for a key box attached to the front gate. I let myself in and found an empty house, pleasant-looking if a hair overdone. Another note on the front table said that the anonymous group that had bailed me out liked to stay anonymous, directed me to food and a spare set of keys, and reminded me that my friends would be there shortly. I wandered into the kitchen, poured myself a bowl of cereal and milk, and wandered through the house with it to pick a bedroom.

Two bedrooms had a tacky beach theme, with generic ocean landscapes on the walls and awful fake starfish on top of their dressers, but the third bedroom was my kind of room. As much as any room in a house could be mine, given that I'd paid loan balances for my entire life instead of a mortgage.

The third bedroom held a simple, low-slung bed, an empty dresser, and an empty but tastefully large closet. I was grateful for the support of whoever had bailed me out, but sad to have to face another empty closet, especially one big enough to hold my stolen wardrobe. This empty closet reminded me of my stripped one, sitting in the middle of my former apartment after the Debt Police ransacked it so hard that every sound I made set off an echo. I lay down on the bed and swore that if I beat the charges, the first thing I would do was buy some fucking clothes. A girl couldn't live in Lanae's borrowed gear forever. I wanted color in my life beyond the infinitely black horizons of punk. I wanted my world, a world full of fuchsia and yellow and orange. I rolled over on my side on the bed and fell asleep immediately.

What do I remember after that? Hugging Lanae when she showed up at the house, giving Audrey the evil eye, even when she explained that she'd had to run away from the security guard, who had headed directly to the car after we went in the building, as if he knew what I drove. Spending weeks waiting to see if Audrey would plead out to fuck Lanae and me over, and feeling like someone had restarted my heart when she didn't. I wasn't up to trusting her, but I didn't have the energy to fight her. We had to focus on the trial.

More so than the trial itself, I remember our group lunch beforehand. According to our lawyer, who had volunteered to defend us because our cause was apparently sexy, there were two kinds of judges in the world. Reasonable people who considered facts and evidence, and high-flying psychos, drunk on the power of the robe, unconcerned with evidence or prior similar cases, disdainful toward Black people and leftists, and ready to convince the jury that we'd fucked up from day one.

I do remember the atmospherics of the trial. All the stiff tan and navy suits the lawyers wore that should have been burned in the 1990s. The judge, stern-looking and robed, using her gavel whenever she couldn't get the lawyers to shut up, just like Judge Judy. The mounting embarrassment, as witness after witness took the stand, at how much our lawyer was right. Everyone had caught us. The security guard pictures of my license plate and of Audrey running away. The debt cop remembered Lanae pouring roofies down his throat. I'd dashed past four sets of security cameras on my way down the alley. We were some of the worst criminals of all time. The courtroom was packed with our fans anyway, and thousands of them who couldn't fit picketed outside. It was hard to walk from the car to the courthouse without being mobbed by people who wanted to hug us for erasing their loans, since the loan company still hadn't found their way around Audrey's hack. After a few grueling weeks of being on trial, one day the judge accepted the verdict from the jury and read it out, announcing that we were acquitted.

"I didn't have any say in this decision," she said, "since I wasn't on the jury. But back in 1990, I had to take out student loans, and it took me two decades to pay them back. The crappy jobs I could get paid the same amount as they do now, but back then it was enough to pay them off. Your generation really got screwed. Good luck to you. And don't ever come back here."

I hugged Audrey and Lanae tightly, like that was the only way we could form a life raft after our boat overturned. We weren't allowed to talk to the jury, but from across the room, when I saw their raised fists and air high fives, I wondered how much of their debt we'd erased. The three of us linked arms to get our way through the crowd, like playing Red Rover if everyone on both teams was forty. I don't remember what we said to each other. But I do remember how I felt: like a hot-air balloon that had just risen to the point where I could see the entire bowl of LA, starting at Griffith Park straight down to the county line, a sea of buildings and sky and infinite, only slightly smoggy possibility.

After two months living together in the house in West Adams, we were free. The three of us gradually fell out of touch after the trial. Audrey spends her days as a glowed-up version of herself, often on TV, where she talks about what she calls "ethical hacking" as a solution to the systemic injustices people are all too happy to never solve. When people ask me political questions about what we did, I tell them to ask her. And then, so far as I can tell, she doesn't answer them. She left LA for the Bay Area, where she reentered the world of the hacking queens. I like thinking of her up there, doing what she really wanted to be doing the whole time. Except now she had carried off one of the most meaningful hacks anyone had ever done. I let go of everything dark I felt about her after she ditched us that night, since she didn't actually fuck us over. She was there when it mattered, in the front seat of the car, silently giddy while we watched her virus run.

Lanae got what she wanted too. To be rich. I had brunch with her a couple of times, and then I mostly saw her in glossy profiles, where she'd suddenly gone from the front woman of a group that sold a few hundred albums a year to one that sold millions. "The godmother of Afro-punk," the music sites called her while they very delicately glossed over the fact that they'd have never interviewed her before. She started giving the kinds of interviews famous people give, interviews where everything was great and she really only ate salmon and broccoli, and of course she hadn't had any work done, she'd just started getting some sleep. Sleep was amazing, it really kept your skin in check.

I couldn't have been happier for her success, but still couldn't put on any of the music she made. One of the greatest tragedies in life is not being able to like your friend's creative work. But then I remembered the good times with my friend who made the weird music I couldn't stand. She could keep recording all that feedback, with the rhythm section that sounded like everyone on earth crashing their cars to the beat, and I'd keep remembering her as our honeypot trap, our roofie queen with the not-quite-perfect technique, and the person who put me up for months at her place after my landlord kicked me out.

The weirdest thing was how quickly they dismantled the student loan system after we were acquitted, as if none of that debt had ever needed to exist in the first place. Bobbie Mae and Willie Sue just quietly went under, like they'd never mattered to begin with. Our copycats hacked into the private loan system. Not all of them got acquitted, but enough of them drew sympathetic judges that they ended up dismantling a lot of that side of the loan industry, too.

After that, most of the people who write news articles revisited the idea of whether student loans should exist, and it became less edgy to say no. It became trendy for colleges to eliminate tuition and renounce the practice of making people take out loans. And then the private loan companies started talking about "risk" and "market trends" and getting around to not feeling like student loans were worth the trouble anymore. After all that, Congress finally got involved when someone claimed that eighteen-year-old freshmen were practically kids, and they passed a bill making student loans illegal, for the sake of the children. It had always been an entire system of useless debt, and because me and my friends had decided to point out by force that it was useless, all of a sudden everyone decided that it was silly it had ever existed.

Some people in my position might have chosen to be bitter about the lengths we were forced to go to in order to get rid of our student loans, but I couldn't. Every time I drove past UCLA or USC and saw happy college students, I felt nothing but joy at knowing they would never have student debt. I savored every single minute of the destruction of the debt police. Those people had thrown all their crystals and their turquoise-ass uniforms into a pile on live television, lit it on fire, and accidentally burned up a park, in true competent cop fashion.

Exactly five years after the trial, and five and a half years after we did it, I finally got what I'd wanted. I left my slightly nicer East Hollywood apartment that morning and drove to a studio on the Paramount lot. I showed the guard ID, found a parking space, and pulled an overstuffed garment bag out of the backseat of my car. Walking on six-inch heels isn't the easiest thing in the world, but I wasn't going to pass up a moment to make an entrance. All that time I'd lived with Lanae had left me with a lingering affection for black. Above black six-inch spike heels I wore a black suit in a new fabric called breathable vinyl, and a fuchsia-colored wig that was a throwback to the one the debt police had stolen from me.

I entered the set, absorbed a round of applause, and dragged my garment bag back to the proper place. I remembered the delicious moment when they'd told me that I could just be an executive producer, and I'd said yes, but also, I'm dressing them. I wanted my life back, and this was it. The smell of the craft table. The crew with walkie-talkies. The row of white trailers outside. The chance to change someone's life with clothes on a bigger scale. I had been dead for years, but this was it. The second trip through the birth canal.

The young actress who'd been picked to play me in the story about our heist greeted me with pleasure. She really did look like me, if you got drunk in the dark and confused me for a supermodel. She had a gentrified version of my face, if its angles and curves had been sanded into something more upscale bistro than diner.

"You got rid of my loans," she said. "You changed everything. I sleep better at night. I can afford my life."

I thought I'd heard all the possible versions of that sentence, but hearing it here, where I'd wanted to be for years, from someone who I'd be costuming for the movie about the craziest thing I ever did, hit different. I teared up.

"That's why I wore this outfit, as tribute," she said.

I took a second look at her. She really had done a decent take on our heist outfits. All black, with a lace eye cover that she'd artfully slung back over her forehead, and the matching black gloves, over a pair of black Nikes that looked very similar to the ones we'd worn.

"That's fabulous, honey," I said. "But your first scene is at Phoenix, so we've got to get you dressed properly."

I unzipped my wardrobe bag and did something that came more naturally to me than drinking water. I told her what she was going to wear.

Acknowledgments

Shout-outs to: Sean deLone, editor extraordinaire · Team Atria · Martha Wydysh and Ellen Levine, my fearless agents · the Bobby Brown album *Don't Be Cruel* · the disco era, in its entirety · the Nicole Perlroth book *This Is How They Tell Me the World Ends* · my student loan debt (RIP) · the Odie Henderson book *Black Caesars and Foxy Cleopatras: A History of Blaxploitation Cinema* · the Los Angeles freeways · the Blaxploitation movie industry · the girls I went clubbing with after our shifts at JCPenney · never, ever being ashamed of being working class